Faye & The Music Fairies

Tutti

Paul Govier-Simpson

Text Copyright ©2015 Lyssa-Jade Woolley (Nee Simpson)
The right of Paul Govier-Simpson to be identified as the author of this work has been asserted by her daughter, Lyssa-Jade Woolley.
All rights reserved.
ISBN: **9798329997002**

This book is sold subject to the condition that it shall not, by way of trade or otherwise, be lent, hired out or otherwise circulated in any form of binding or cover other than that in which it is published.
No part of this publication may be reproduced, stored in a retrieval system, transmitted in any form of means (electronic, mechanical, photocopying, recording or otherwise) without the written permission of Lyssa-Jade Woolley, Copyright holder.

Illustrations Copyright ©2024 Joelle Henry

OTHER BOOKS IN THE FAYE & THE MUSIC FAIRIES SERIES

1 The Clef Crystal

2 Scales

3 Dee Sharp

4 Woodwind

5 Crescendo

6 Tutti

ACKNOWLEDGEMENTS

As always, I need to thank Hannah for proofreading, especially since you got the last two books done in record time! Thank you for being a part of this series - I know mum originally wanted you to be a part of what she was calling the "inner circle" (much like her own version of the Circle of Five!) whereby she was going to give a close group of friends a copy of the books to read and give feedback, and so it means a lot that you were still able to be a part of the process.

Jo, what can I say that I haven't already said in the last 5 books? Thank you doesn't quite seem enough for all the hard work you have put in creating these fantastic covers - you've been able to create what I can see in my head, just from me giving you a brief description via messenger! Your talent is incredible, and I am so happy you answered my Facebook ad when I was first looking for a designer!

Lastly, I need to thank the most important person of all…
Paul.
Thank you, you mad woman, for giving us this beautiful set of books, that we can not just enjoy, but also feel closer to you (especially for those readers that knew you!)
Without you, these books would not exist, and in my humble (and not biased whatsoever!) opinion, that would be an absolute shame!

A Note From The Authors Daughter

I am writing this with tears in my eyes.
Tears of joy that I have finally fulfilled my promise to my mum just before she passed, but also tears of sadness that this is the final book.
There are a few questions left unanswered in this book that I wish I could go back in time and ask, however all I am able to tell you is that Mum did begin to write a prequel; the story of Landler and Forlana as children, and who Dee Sharp was before she became the evil enchantress that we all know from these books.
I have toyed with the idea of publishing her unfinished work, but do not know whether to publish it as is, and let you, the readers fill in your own endings, or do I try and finish it myself?

What would you all like to be done? let me know either personally, or via the Faye & The Music Fairies Facebook page (that is, if anyone would actually like to read the prequel!)

Mum - as always, this is for you - we finally did it!
I'm sorry it has taken me so long, but you of all people would understand why.
Love you always my butterfly Fairy.

Lyssa -x-

CHAPTER 1

Landler sat grimly astride Scales, silently willing the little dragon to go faster, even while knowing he mustn't tax him.

The Maestro, summoned from his study by the news that a Beamer had crash-landed outside the Quarters, looked drawn and exhausted, but Tanto, told to fetch his master with all speed, failed to notice.

"Please will you come, Maestro. It's Landler's Beamer, Brand; he looks to be in a terrible state! … And Polka's very ill!"

Monody, lurching from one crisis to another, felt in a pretty terrible state himself, but Tanto would not have guessed it from the calm reply.

"Of course, Tanto. Thank you for letting me know."

Message delivered, Tanto left to see what other errands may need doing.

Once he'd arrived at the Quarters, it hadn't taken the Maestro more than a few seconds to assess the situation, for, after projecting that one thought of Polka crying, engulfed in sadness to Landler, Brand had collapsed, unconscious.

Landler had rushed to his friend in horror, and by the time Monody arrived on the scene, he looked every bit drained as his master felt!

"He's still breathing!"

"Good."

Landler turned in anguish. "Maestro, do you know about the infusion?"

Fanfare broke in. "Flame berries and nectar? Yes… Forlana told me. I'll look after him, Landler, don't worry."

Fanfare dashed out to get some Fairies to start making it immediately, while Landler looked round for Scales.

The little dragon had, in fact, heard the crash outside the doors, and, alerting the Fairies, had helped open them and drag Brand inside.

He'd then gone back to close the huge, heavy doors, and was now busy fanning the remaining wisps of mist out of the air vent.

"Landler," the Maestro began, in his gentlest voice, "I'm afraid you can't…"

But at this point, Scales had come over to them.

"Scales! Polka's sick - I <u>have</u> to go!"

"Of course, Landler."

"Just a moment!" The stern voice of the Composition Magician halted them both in their tracks.

Monody looked at Landler's pleading face, then at Scales' curious expression and sighed. He ought to forbid the pair of them to go <u>anywhere</u>, but he was wise enough to know that, in <u>this</u> instance, arguing would be futile.

Shaking his head slightly, he gave in.

"Go find your mask and tank, Landler."

The tall Fairy rushed to fetch it.

"Scales," Monody looked him in the eye. "You <u>cannot</u> rush to get him there! If we lose <u>you</u>, we lose all - do you understand?"

The little dragon looked serious and nodded.

"You'll stay at the Red Barn for at least two days… AT LEAST! You'll eat and you'll rest… PROMISE ME!"

"I promise," replied Scales in a small voice because the Maestro sounded almost angry with him.

As if reading his thoughts, the Maestro made himself relax and smile, as he patted the little dragon.

"I'm not cross <u>with</u> you… I'm worried <u>for</u> you; can you see the difference?"

"Yes, Maestro," he nodded, much happier now. "I see, but I want to help Polka, and <u>she</u> needs Landler."

"Yes, she does. Now, have you chewed enough Flame Rock?"

"Yes, Maestro. But the bag I left in my Quarters is nearly empty now, too!"

"Don't worry," Monody smiled a secret smile, "I know where I can get more!"

Landler ran back in and skidded to a halt in front of his master.

"GO!" Monody gripped his arm in farewell. "Look after Polka; we'll look after Brand."

Landler took a long look at the Beamer, then looked back to the Maestro and nodded, grimly.

He clambered up onto Scales' back.

The heavy doors were heaved open, Scales helping where he

could, and after one crouched spring the little dragon disappeared into the mist.

The doors having been closed once more; Monody turned his attention to Brand. They had no Beamer <u>Medics</u> at Scores Hall, for the butterflies seldom became ill, but there were, of course, Beamers working in the rooms that Faye and Peri had visited on their stay at the Hall, so, as Fanfare returned, Monody said, "Sorry to send you off on another errand, my friend, but do you think it would be a good idea to get Brindisi down here? She can communicate with Brand in ways we cannot."

"Yes, yes, of course. I'll fetch her." And he was off again.

Monody felt the need to sit down for five minutes. The day had barely begun and he'd already had a meeting with the Circle to tell them of his idea, then implementing that idea had very nearly drained him of <u>all</u> his powers, and <u>now</u>, he sat watching a magical creature whom he'd admired and respected, hovering on the brink of death, because he had been desperate enough to try the impossible so he could tell his best friend how sorely he was needed.

How many more sacrifices would have to be made before they could end this malice and evil once and for all?

Had the Maestro but known it, Landler, now well into his journey with Scales flying steadily, was thinking exactly the same thing.

CHAPTER 2

"Ouch!" Faye banged her head on Peri's knee as they landed, not in the soft grass and flowers of the Mezzo Meadow, but on a hard, wooden floor in…

"Scores Hall!" Faye cried in amazement, recognising the portraits of famous Fairy composers (and some Human ones, too!) which hung all around the walls.

"Why?…" but the question died on her lips as she saw Peri's face, staring beyond her, in total astonishment.

Faye turned around to see, then her mouth, quite literally, fell open… for there, in the main hall, were dozens of Human boys and girls, all looking equally astonished and all, Faye guessed, wearing Clef Crystals, some of which could be seen, and others showing just the chain, the Crystal hidden beneath tee shirts and tops.

At that moment there was a noise as the Maestro arrived with more haste than dignity, having run from the Quarters in response to the message: "Come quick, the hall is full of Humans!"

Monody went to the large staging area at the front, heaving slightly as he went up the steps. He took a deep breath then said, "Can you all hear me?"

He projected his golden voice right to the back of the hall; everyone nodded silently.

"First of all, welcome to Scores Hall; for those of you who have not been <u>here</u> before, this is the centre of musical learning here in Octavia."

Some people looked a bit bewildered, leading Faye and Peri to realise that not <u>everyone</u> had been honoured with a visit to the hall.

"Secondly," the Maestro continued, "I must apologise for the, er… slightly rough manner in which some of you arrived."

Here, he glanced inquiringly at Faye and Peri - they grinned at him and saw the answering twinkle in his eyes.

"You see, I have never tried to bring <u>all</u> of you here <u>at the same time</u>, but the fact is, we need you <u>all</u> now in a way we never have before!"

Several of the children looked around at each other, but Peri looked at the rich purple velvet curtains… which were all closed.

"Does it feel like night-time to you?" she asked Faye, quietly.

"No…" began Faye, then she, too, noticed that no one could see outside.

"It's here?" Peri murmured.

Faye nodded, then turned her attention back to the Maestro.

"I'm aware it will take a little time to settle, so food and drink will be brought in directly, and then I'll do my best to explain what is happening."

Monody inclined his head, then left the stage and went to open the doors to admit Melodia and her team, bearing refreshments.

As everyone was milling about, Faye and Peri seized the opportunity to edge their way to the doors through which the Maestro had gone and were not surprised when Fanfare suddenly appeared and said, "Ah, good. Follow me, please."

The girls slipped out, unnoticed, and went with the little herald to Monody's study: he was there, waiting for them.

"Maestro!" The two girls ran to him, and he took the hand of each.

"Faye! Peri! Thank goodness." He smiled at them, indicating two small lilac chairs, between which nestled a delicate table, laden with food and drink.

They both sat, took the food that Fanfare offered, then, as he left quietly, turned their attention back to the Composition Magician.

"You didn't get hurt, did you?"

"No," said Faye, laughing. "It was more the shock of landing on something hard when we were expecting the Meadow!"

"Yes, I apologise for that. There was no way to let you know beforehand, but it's too dangerous to land anywhere <u>outside</u>, at present!"

"The Woodwind… is it here?" asked Peri, already knowing the answer.

The Maestro nodded, sadly.

"What about the others?" Faye asked, anxiously.

Monody knew, at once, whom she meant.

"Forlana is running things at Cadence Falls, with her usual efficiency,"

Peri grinned at him.

"… and Landler has just gone back to the Red Barn on Scales."

"Scales?" Faye was delighted that her friend was able to be useful.

"Yes, the Woodwind doesn't seem to affect him in the same way as it does... others."

The two girls, quick to notice his change of tone, asked for an explanation.

By the time he'd told them about Polka... and Brand, both the girls were frantic.

"What can <u>we</u> do?" Faye said, jumping up.

"Is there another way for us to get there?" Peri joined her.

"What about..."

He held up his hand for silence.

"Believe me, I know how you feel. I also wish I could be there to help Polka, but <u>we</u> are needed elsewhere. We have the <u>whole</u> of Octavia to save!"

The tone in which this was said made them sit down once more.

"Very shortly, I must go and address all these very confused children in the main hall and explain why you have all been called at the same time!"

"Of <u>course</u>!" Faye suddenly exclaimed. "We're not the only ones!"

Peri frowned at her.

"Don't you see, Peri? Kids who are good at music get called into Octavia all the time. They each get their own Mentor, like we have Landler and Forlana, and they each go to a different village and help with different things... er... is that right?" She turned to look at the Maestro, who was beaming at her with approval.

"Yes, Faye; that's exactly right. It's <u>very</u> unusual for two children to be called to the same place at the same time... though I have known of it before..." He broke off, as if looking back through time.

The girls stared at him, he looked up and continued, smoothly.

"But, then, you two had a very unusual link." He was, of course, referring to the fact that the first time Peri had come to Octavia was to save Faye's life!

"So..." began Peri, slowly, "all those kids out there thought <u>they</u> were the only ones?"

Monody nodded.

"Oh!" said Faye. "No wonder they all looked so lost and bewildered."

"Exactly! So now you see why I must go and speak to them all, now that they've eaten and rested, and explain what they're all doing here."

"What _are_ we all doing here?" asked Peri.

"You'll have to be patient," laughed the Maestro, teasing them, "I don't think I have the energy to try and explain it all twice, so, now we've had a chance to catch up, let's go back to the main hall, and I'll let you _all_ in on the master plan!

CHAPTER 3

As he flamed away a large patch of Woodwind, Scales saw, at last, the huge doors of the Red Barn in the distance, far below him.

The mist was beginning to thicken now, and both Scales and Landler knew that if they didn't land soon, they would find it almost impossible to gauge their direction.

With a final burst of speed, Scales zoomed down before the swirling Woodwind could close around them again, his powerful wings clearing some of the nearer clouds away from them.

When they landed, (Scales, having managed with amazing accuracy, to place himself squarely in the area leading to the Barn,) the great doors, (as they already knew) were closed against them.

Scales, having practised this twice before now, gave a mighty bang with his foreleg and, sure enough, he could hear scraping as the large wooden bars were slid back on the inside.

Scales pushed hard against the doors, and they opened just enough to let him squeeze in… and, as before, he quickly turned and closed it, fanning the Woodwind back outside with his wings.

Landler, barely waiting for the little dragon to finish his manoeuvre, flung himself down from his mount, ripped off both helmet and tank, and looked around, frantically.

Corona saw him and silently pointed towards the infirmary.

Landler ran as fast as he could, then skidded to a halt, as, in the first cubicle he came to, he saw Viola trying to spoon an infusion of daffodil and poppy into her patient.

"Landler!" she looked up. "However did you get here?"

"Scales," he said, shortly. "What's wrong!"

"We think Polka may have inhaled a small amount of the Woodwind, during the rescue from Pavane Villa… You know that cough she had? That must have been the beginning. Talk to her, Landler; she's convinced herself that you left because you don't love her, anymore."

"WHAT?" Landler sank onto a nearby stool, his legs suddenly

turned to jelly.

"I know," Viola went to him and patted his shoulder in sympathy, "but it's all a part of the illness."

She led him to the edge of Polka's bed and sat him down there. He looked down at the sleeping Fairy who was moaning and shaking her head.

"I'm here, dearest; I'm here."

He took her hand and held it as if he would never let her go.

Satisfied that her patient was in the best possible care, Viola quietly left.

Scales was sitting down in the exact spot where Landler had left him.

"Scales!" Viola ran over to him and patted his cheek. "How are you feeling?"

"A bit tired, but I'm fine, thank you," the little dragon replied, "but <u>very</u> hungry."

"Of course you are!" Viola led him to a large, empty storage room, saying, "Would this be big enough for you to sleep in?"

"Oh, of course! Only…" the little dragon looked at her, "could I be in the main hall? I could sleep in a corner, I don't take up <u>too</u> much room!"

"Of course you can," smiled Viola.

"It's just that I like to be around people, and I need to know how Polka is, and make sure Landler is alright, too."

"That's fine, Scales," said Viola, filling him in on all that had happened, as she led him to the corner of the main hall that didn't have any doors leading to other sections.

"Will this do?"

"Perfect," smiled Scales, happily.

Corona had gone to organise food and water the second she was free, so it wasn't long before the little dragon was munching away, having had a long drink.

Viola took the opportunity to fetch some old blankets and covers from the linen room and returned with them, just as Scales finished.

She spread the covers all around him on the floor.

"Ooh! That's lovely!" He snuggled down into the softness. "Thank you, Viola."

The little dragon gave a mighty yawn, tucked his tail under his head and was fast asleep in minutes.

Viola stroked him gently, then went to return to her duties.

***

Monody, having left a whole collection of frightened and bemused children in the hall to mull over his plan for them, made his way wearily back to the Magical Creatures Quarters, and from there, into Scales' private quarters, which were just off the main room where Brand still lay.

Deciding he would fetch the Flame Rock sacks and fill them, first and foremost, gave him something practical to do, rather than worrying about everything and every<u>one</u> else!

It was not generally known, but when Scales had first hatched, Monody had sent two of his most trusted colleagues back into the Crescendo Range to not only search once more for the missing dragons, but also to collect Flame Rock so that, as the baby dragon grew, they would be able to teach him how to Flame; (a task the adult dragons would normally have undertaken.)

Monody had kept the supply in a large chest in his rooms because, what with all the <u>other</u> duties that came with being Composition Magician, he had not yet had the chance to begin the instruction.

<u>Now</u>, of course, Monody was grateful to have a spare supply, as he would not risk anyone on a trip to the Range... even <u>with</u> the masks; it was just too dangerous.

He saw the empty sacks lying as Scales had described, picked them up and swung them over his shoulder; but in doing so, something fell out and clattered across the floor.

Monody turned to idly glance at it, then dropped the sacks from suddenly lifeless hands, for there, gleaming softly in front of him, was...

The Draconis Stone!

With trembling fingers, the Maestro picked it up and examined it. There was no mistaking it for, apart from the green and blue veins that shimmered through the silver, there was the same sequence of letters that sat around the Circle of Fifths plaque in the special 'study'.

C, G, D, A, E... The very ones they used to unlock the secret chamber for the Circle of Five to meet!

It would have been beautiful to behold in any circumstances, but in the hands of the Composition Magician, it positively trembled with power!

Throwing caution to the winds, Monody picked up his robes and ran, like one possessed, back to the corridors of the hall, yelling for Fanfare!

Several Fairies stared in amazement as he rushed past, nearly colliding with Fanfare, as <u>he</u> came pelting round a corner in his haste to get to his master.

"Get the Circle - get the Circle... NOW!"

Fanfare glanced around fearfully. Had his master lost the plot to be yelling about the Circle in public?!

But he said, "At once, Maestro!" then watched as the usually stately and elegant Fairy hurtled towards the 'study' where the Circle of Five met.

CHAPTER 4

Landler sat, exactly where Viola had left him, on the bed where Polka lay, restless and fevered.

So far, she had woken up abruptly, twice, sobbing, 'He doesn't love me - <u>why</u> doesn't he love me?'

Landler cradled her in his arms, rocking her gently, saying over and over again, "It's alright, my dearest; I am here, and I love you so very much."

She looked vaguely up at him, then with a tiny glimmer of recognition, her eyes widened, and she smiled briefly, then once more, drifted away in sleep.

The first time this had happened, Landler had been in a fair way thinking her cured, but the next time she awoke, it was very clear she remembered nothing of their previous encounter, and Landler had to go through it all over again.

The third time it happened, Landler began to cry silently, and as Viola came in, she stood for a second, her heart going out to Landler in his grief. When he noticed her, he did not attempt to brush the tears away.

"Viola… I feel so helpless… is there <u>nothing</u> that will help?"

Viola thought for a moment.

"I'm not certain, Landler, but I'll go and consult the older medical books and see if there's anything there. Now, please go and eat something, or else you'll be no good to Polka when she <u>does</u> get better."

This was said with such a positive note that Landler actually rose and went to get some food in the main barn, before he realised he wasn't in fact hungry.

He glanced over to the corner, feeling suddenly guilty that he hadn't been out to check on the little dragon since they arrived!

However, Scales seemed happy enough chatting to Brio, who had come to enquire after Polka.

Landler was about to go over and join them, having poured

himself some Lupin tea, which was all he could manage, when Viola came running in, calling him. This made everyone in the main barn look up, as Polka was a great favourite with them all.

"Landler, come, sit down!"

He sped across to her, nearly spilling his tea in his haste.

"What is it? Have you found something?"

"Just one paragraph from long ago, telling some Fairies who were fading through evil magic, rather than old age. It recommends crushing the leaves of a plant, commonly thought to be a weed, in an infusion! The problem is, this weed only grows underwater."

Landler jumped up, yelling, "the Diapason Plant! I know where they grow!" Then he slumped down again.

"But I have no way of letting Forlana know we <u>need</u> it! It grows in the Pizzicato Pool, just outside Cadence Falls; Peri got some for Faye when she was so sick. I wonder if the Maestro has called them yet? Only Peri knows exactly <u>where</u> it is!"

He stopped and looked at Viola in anguish.

"I can't tell them, and I can't <u>get</u> there, unless…"

He glanced across at Scales, but the little dragon was fast asleep again.

"No, Landler; not even for Polka," Viola said, sadly. "He's exhausted. Oh, I've no doubt he'd go if you asked him, but what would happen if he failed halfway to Cadence Falls? You'd both die… and <u>then</u> what would Polka do?"

Landler looked at her - tears streaming down his face.

"But what will <u>I</u> do, if I lose Polka?"

Viola put her arm around him and shook her head, sadly.

"We'll think of <u>something</u>, Landler; we <u>must</u>!"

In their shared sadness, neither of them noticed when Brio had left…

***

Considering all the dramas they had come through, Presto thought Forlana and Shawm had done a good job of organising life at Cadence Falls.

The Treatment Centre at Landler's old house was only half-full, and everyone there was being taken good care of.

The food supply was lasting well, thanks to Shawm's foresight in getting all the fruit and vegetables picked and stored.

They'd dealt with a Cascade without any major injuries, and the masks and oxy-tanks had worked very well indeed.

All they'd had to do was keep fanning the Woodwind out the way, so they could see!

And now, there was constantly someone on watch at the windows by the main doors to report on the state of the Woodwind and any more Cascades that may come.

Forlana, always at her best during a crisis, managed everything with crisp efficiency, and if some Fairies (including Presto) found her a bit scary at times, especially if she was angry about something, they all knew, without doubt, that Forlana had their best interests at heart.

They were now sitting, as they did every evening, at the table she and the Maestro had shared, listening to whoever was playing.

Presto (having been told about the mystery patient) was pleased to see that Dale Van Clef now came into the main room to join in the evening's entertainment. He wouldn't come out, still, during the day, but this was progress indeed! And the strange thing was that, of all the people he had to sit with, he chose Crumhorn, Sackbut, Lilt and Dash.

At first, Forlana was astonished, but Presto thought he understood.

"They were all in the same boat, Forlana, for although it might have <u>looked</u> as though Dale was there by choice, it's pretty obvious now that he wasn't. They're all glad to be free of Dee Sharp, and that creates a bond between them. The two Goblins only seem to have been there for a few months, but if you listen to him talk, I think that Dale has probably lived in that dead wood right from the beginning! But he <u>is</u> starting to improve… just look at him!"

It was true; Crumhorn and Sackbut sat clapping (not always in time, unfortunately) while Dale played away on his oboe.

The Goblins had also improved; they no longer fell asleep instantly if music was being played (although Sackbut still had a tendency to nod off if the tune was slow and gentle,) and the expression on everyone's face who <u>wasn't</u> playing was happy and contented.

In fact, it had given Presto an idea which, much to his surprise,

Forlana had agreed to.

"Suppose I took a couple of people up to the Treatment Centre and we played for the patients? Might help them."

"It might, indeed!" replied Forlana, after a moment's thought. "Only volunteers, mind! I'm not forcing anyone out in <u>that</u> unless it's a Cascade!"

Presto, rising, said, "Of course, Forlana, Thank you."

He put the plan to the Gnomes first, intending to ask the Fairies later, but when every single Gnome volunteered (including the two Goblins, even though they couldn't play… or sing!) Presto chose Jig and Reel first, promising the others they'd all get a turn eventually.

So far, he'd done two trips and Fretta reported that while small, she <u>had</u> noticed a slight improvement in her patient's spirits.

Forlana was just asking Presto who he intended on choosing next when Stem, who was on window-watch, called out, "Something's coming! Flying, I think, through the mist, heading this way!"

"Scales! It must be!"

Forlana and Presto rose and ran towards the large doors.

"Let us know when he lands, Stem. We won't open til the last minute!"

Several of the Gnomes rushed to help.

"Now!" yelled Stem, and they all began to pull on one of the large doors… it seemed much harder than usual, Forlana thought… as though Scales wasn't really pushing from his side, but at last they got it open to admit…

"Brio!" Forlana cried in amazement, as the Beamer virtually fell in at an awkward angle and crash-landed by the nearest table.

Everyone jumped out the way, and while the Gnomes made haste to shut the great door again, Forlana rushed to Brio's side. He wore no bridle, harness <u>or</u> saddle!

Forlana was confused.

"Where's Landler?" she asked.

Brio projected two very strong pictures to her. The first was of Polka lying, white-faced in a bed, whilst Landler sat, holding her hand, silently weeping. The second was of a strange plant, growing underwater, the like of which Forlana had only seen <u>once</u> before.

"I understand, Brio; thank you."

She patted the Beamers' head, aware of the huge sacrifice he had made to get there, blind and unaided. She sensed his relief, as he seemed to make one more colossal effort, before he closed his eyes, laid down his head… and slept where he was.

She turned and felt all eyes on her, and, sighing as she rose, said, "Polka is gravely ill. The Woodwind must have got to her."

A gasp went up. She heard Presto come to stand beside her.

"It's alright; Landler is with her."

The gasp changed to a sigh of relief, echoed by Presto.

"<u>But</u>…" went on Forlana, "we need to find a Diapason Plant, which only grows underwater, in the Pizzicato Pool, to save her."

The Fairies and Gnomes looked at each other in dismay.

Apart from the fact that none of the Fairies could swim <u>under</u>water, because of their wings; (the Gnomes couldn't swim at all!) the Ondulandi now had a new Olani who may not welcome intruders.

Forlana turned to Presto.

"There's only one person who can help us, and I don't even know if the Maestro has called her here yet! Besides which, <u>how</u> are we going to let her know?"

CHAPTER 5

"Do you think this… what's he called?"

"Maestro," Faye put in, quickly, before Peri could snap a reply back.

"This Maestro, then, do you think his plan will work?"

The boy wore a worried expression; his sandy hair and flushed complexion made him look more nervous than anything else, but Faye sensed something else was bothering him.

"What's really wrong, Ryan?" she asked.

"Tempo's in Galliard," he said quietly, not looking up.

"Who's Tempo?" Scott, the tall, bossy-sounding boy asked.

"My… my Mentor. I don't know if… if h's…"

"Look, try not to worry too much," said Peri with about as much sympathy as Forlana would have used. "Yes, we know some Fairy folk were injured and worse, but an awful lot were inside when the Woodwind arrived, so they must be alright!" She looked at Faye for confirmation.

"It really is too early to tell yet, Ryan. Our mentors are not here, either." Faye cast a warning look at Peri; they may not be there, but the girls knew exactly where they were and what they were doing!

"Well," cried Scott, standing up, bored now the attention was on someone else, "I don't think this plan will work out at all; how can it, when we're all at different levels and play different instruments. I think…"

But whatever Scott thought they never found out, for at that moment, Faye screamed in pain, put her hands to her head… and collapsed!

Peri saw Melodia rushing over, and between them, they half-carried, half-dragged Faye outside.

"To the Maestro's study!" gasped Melodia as she tried to hold the heavy door open and haul Faye through it.

They managed to get Faye into the study and onto the little chaise lounge in the corner, where she lay moaning and rubbing her temples.

Melodia, after pouring some water for Faye, went off to find the Maestro, so Peri sat fearfully, wondering if Faye was going to succumb to that illness she'd had before, which had nearly killed her!

Luckily, before too long, Faye managed to open her eyes, blink a little, and look round. When she saw Peri's face, she realised at once what her friend was thinking and cried, "It's alright, Peri! I'm not getting sick, please don't worry."

Peri took her hand.

"Whatever was that?"

"I'm not sure," began Faye, slowly, "but I think Brio was trying to connect with me - it felt like him."

"What did he say?"

"He just showed me a very faint picture of a plant," said Faye.

"A plant?"

"And then, right in the middle of that, another picture burst into my head - that one really hurt!" she winced, "because I think I got it twice!"

"What was it?"

Faye looked at her with troubled eyes.

"Polka, really sick and Landler, heart broken." She swallowed hard. "It... It almost felt like it came from Landler; it's only happened once before, but I did hear Landler's voice when I really needed him... so he must really need me, now!" She jumped up. "But what can I do? The Woodwind is here!"

Peri was thinking fast.

"This plant you saw, was there anything else in the picture?"

"Um... I don't know... it wasn't very clear. I mean it looked like it was surrounded by water, but that can't be right, can it?"

"Yes, it can!" Peri sprang to her feet. "Come on, we need to find the Maestro!"

However, as they ran out into the corridor, they suddenly heard a great roaring and trumpeting coming from the distance. As one, every Fairy stopped and listened.

"What was that?" asked Faye.

Melodia, who had been about to return with a tray of refreshments for the girls, having been unable to locate her master, paused and said, "It almost sounds like... no, it can't be!"

And with that cryptic statement, she put down the tray on a nearby table, and ran off in another direction.

The two girls sipped their drinks and stared at each other.

Then, round the corner came Fanfare and two other professors, all wearing masks and oxy-tanks, running towards the great harp-shaped doors. Four burly Fairies heaved them open a little ways, then the three ran out, then the doors were shut.

Faye and Peri put their drinks down and went in search of the Maestro; they found him, coming out of a study they'd not previously been in.

"Maestro!" Faye said quickly, "Polka's very ill; Landler managed to make contact with me, somehow - Brio, too!"

"We need a Diapason Plant!" broke in Peri, anxious to get to the point, "but I don't know <u>how</u> I can get to the Pizzicato Pool!"

"I may have just solved that problem," beamed Monody; then he paused, as what Faye had said suddenly sank in…

"Pokla's sick?! We must act quickly, come with me!"

They ran after him and nearly missed him diving into a cupboard as they rounded the corner.

"Right! Peri, hold this!" He handed her what looked like the very bubblehead and chestpiece she'd worn on her trip to see the Olani, last time!

While Peri was examining it, the Maestro whispered something to Faye… Peri caught something about 'Dale', but she wasn't really listening.

Next came the masks and oxy-tanks.

"Put these on; do what you have to do to save Polka, then go back to Cadence Falls and wait for me there."

"But how are we going to <u>get</u> there?" asked Faye.

A roar sounded, much meaner now, and the Maestro, seeing their startled expressions, grinned at them.

"I found, or rather <u>Scales</u> found the missing Draconis Stone… I've called the lost Dragons of the Crescendo Range! They're back!"

CHAPTER 6

Faye and Peri sat, knees pressed tightly against the sides of a huge, purple dragon. They'd barely had time to gasp in amazement, before the Maestro had thrust them up onto the massive foreleg, from which they had to then scramble up to the dragon's neck. Monody had told them exactly where to sit and how to hold on. They'd barely got settled when the dragon suddenly took off!

Faye and Peri had to trust that he knew where he was going; and the voice in which he had acknowledged the Maestro's request to fly the girls to Cadence Falls had been bright and respectful, but it was still slightly scary to be flying on an unknown dragon into the thick, green mist.

Neither of the girls now had <u>any</u> idea of where they were, for the Woodwind grew thicker every minute and swirled around them in great, green clouds: Faye couldn't tell if she were over water, forest or mountain!

From the slight shifting behind her, she guessed Peri felt exactly the same.

Despite the dragon flaming mist out of the way, the journey seemed to take much longer than usual, but Faye thought that was because she couldn't see any landmarks by which to time the journey, the way she did when Fanfare and the bluebirds flew her in the Maestro's carriage.

The dragon suddenly caught the sound of rumbling water and back-winged violently. The two girls shot forward, barely clinging on, as the dragon stopped short, <u>just</u> in front of the Warehouse doors! Faye and Peri had started to slip and slide down the large beasts back, when one door was dragged open and two masked figures rushed out to catch them!

They literally fell onto the arms of Dash and Lilt, (the only two Gnomes willing to come out and face a <u>very</u> large, and unknown dragon!)

As they were then set on their feet, a figure waved them into the Warehouse... a figure with flailing arm gestures, who could only be...

"Forlana!" Peri yelled through her mask; the Fairy gave her a thumbs up sign and pointed inside.

The girls obeyed and saw Forlana look up at the dragon through the swirling mist, gesturing round the back of the Warehouse where there was a large lean-to, big enough to provide <u>some</u> shelter for him. The dragon nodded and moved off.

Dash went off to get a bucket of scraps and took it to the back window - the dragon would be hungry!

Forlana turned quickly and went inside, so the large door could be closed. Faye noticed everyone else stood well back, in case the tendrils of green mist should touch them. Two Gnomes with large leaf fans beat the mist out again towards the closing door.

Once safe, the party stripped off their masks and tanks and the three girls hugged each other tightly.

Shawm came up, and, without even saying 'hello' gasped, "W... where did you get tha... that dragon from?"

Faye smiled at him.

"Scales found the Draconis Stone, and the Maestro called the lost dragons with it. They're back... <u>all</u> of them!"

The whole place erupted with massive shouts and cheers; this was the best news they'd had in ages!

Peri smiled quietly, but then turned to Forlana to say, "I need to get to the Pizzicato Pool as quickly as possible. Polka's sick and I have to find another..."

" ... Diapason Plant!" Forlana finished for her. "But how do <u>you</u> already know that?"

Faye touched her arm, gently.

"I had a <u>double</u> telepathic message; one from Brio and the other from... Landler."

"Of course!" Forlana cried. "I remember you telling me you could hear Landler's voice, when you and Brio were injured in the Cacophony Wood."

"Forlana," Peri cut in, "sorry to interrupt, but I really need to get going!"

Forlana frowned.

"The only problem is, Peri, the Olani has... changed, since you were there last time, and I don't know if the new one will let you in!"

Peri stared, wide-eyed at her. She had liked and respected the

Olani and wasn't prepared to hear she had gone.

Forlana nodded at her understanding, thought for a moment, then said, "What did you do with the Sospiro Shell the Olani gave you?"

"I left it at Landler's... Oh!" She put her hands to her mouth. "Everything's been moved since then - I don't know where it'll be now!"

"That's alright, I do!" Forlana replied, crisply.

"Presto!" She called the tall Fairy over. "Do you feel like walking up to Polka's new place and fetching the small wooden box with the oak leaves carved round it?"

"The one I made for Polka's odds and ends?"

"That's the one."

"Of course!" He smiled at the two girls. "I won't be long."

He went over to the barrel of masks and tanks that stood by the door, put a set on, then waved as Shawm and Dal heaved open the big door a very little, so that Presto could slip out into the Woodwind.

"Now, Peri," Forlana went on, briskly, "I need you to eat and drink, whilst I explain what you'll need to do to get into the Pool without an invite!"

Faye left them to it, and wandered over to where Dash and Lilt were sitting with the two Goblins, trying to unravel a very tangled pile of ropes.

"Hello, Faye!" Dash got up and offered her his seat.

"Hi Dash, - I was just wondering, er... do you know where Dirge... I mean, Dale is?"

Dash looked at her, doubtfully.

"Well, um..."

"It's alright, the Maestro wants me to talk to him. He's explained, and I promise I'll go gently. It's just that... I know his brother, you see."

"Oh, well, of course, Faye, if the Maestro says it's alright... he's in there."

Dash pointed to the curtained area over on the other side.

Faye nodded and made her way quietly to the old and faded curtain.

CHAPTER 7

Faye listened carefully; she could hear the sounds of something being picked up and put down, accompanied by a soft humming.

She pulled the curtain aside, slowly and gently.

Dale glanced up and saw a young girl, smiling at him.

"Hello," she said softly. "What a lovely oboe - it is yours?" (The Maestro had told her that this was the best way to begin a conversation with him.)

Dale looked up from the section he was polishing and beamed at her.

"Yes! It's mine - come and see!"

Faye spent the next ten minutes listening to him tell her all about his beloved oboe, before she dared venture onto the next topic of conversation.

"I've just come from a really nice place where everybody can learn to play instruments. There's lots of teachers who are really kind and loads of instruments to practise on… I play piano…"

"Do you?" Dale looked at her with interest.

"Yes, and at first I didn't like having to practise every day, but now I'm better at it." She smiled at him. "My friend, Peri, is really clever; she plays the flute <u>and</u> the violin - though not at the same time!"

Dale laughed with her - he really liked this child; she was different from the Gnomes and Fairies.

Faye went on, carefully, "Peri loves music, but her <u>brother</u>, Ben…" She paused, "<u>he</u> thinks music is for girls, he only likes football and swimming." she ended quietly, watching his puzzled expression.

"Brother." He said the word slowly.

She waited.

"Brother… I have friends," he said, uncertainly.

Dale suddenly reached under his pillow and brought out the last thing Faye expected… a scrap of Polka's handkerchief that Faye had been carrying during her trip to the Cacophony Wood!

Faye smiled at him.

"I hope you'll let me be your friend, too."

He offered it to her as if sealing the bargain.

"Friends," he nodded, absently, and went back to polishing his oboe.

Faye left him to it, pulling the curtains across as she went.

Well, she'd done what the Maestro had asked her to, in the hastily whispered chat they'd had on the way to the dragon.

"Just mention brothers if you can, Faye. Don't push it - just drop the word into the conversation... remember to start with the oboe!"

"How?" Faye had asked blankly.

"Oh, you'll think of a way; Dale needs to remember!"

And then they were up on the dragon and away. On the journey, she was able to plan a vague idea of bringing Peri's brother into it, somehow, and it seemed to have worked!

She had been worried that Dirge/Dale would recognise her as his former mistress's prisoner, but the Maestro had pointed out that he, too, had now escaped Dee Sharp, so it was unlikely he would feel anything but sympathy if he should remember, which was very doubtful.

She had done her best and now they would just have to wait and see.

As she came out into the main building, she heard her name called in a faint voice in her head. It seemed to be coming from nearby!

She stopped Minima, who happened to be passing and said, "Is Brio here?"

"Yes, didn't Forlana tell you?" replied Minima, gently. "Through there; he's in a bad way, though."

Faye dashed off in the direction the Fairy had given her and found a partition off the side corridor, where they had taken the Beamer to treat him.

Brio was grey from head to toe, his once beautiful colours dull and lifeless. He was attached to a large bottle of the nectar and Flame berry infusion that he'd had before when he and Faye had returned from the Cacophony Wood.

Faye, with tears streaming down her face, went to kneel beside him, stroking his head gently.

"Oh! Brio! You're so brave, coming here alone. Why did you do it?"

The Beamer projected the same faint picture as before... Polka and Landler.

"Peri's all ready to go and get the Diapason Plant... you may as well have saved Polka's life... thank you."

She laid her head against him, sending as much love and strength as she could from her heart.

She soon sensed he was asleep again, and getting up quietly, she dried her eyes on the scrap of Polka's handkerchief and went back.

The large door was just opening to admit Presto, carrying a box, and once he'd got his mask and tank off, it was obvious he'd run all the way!

Forlana went up to him, took the box... then punched him hard on the shoulder.

"Idiot! Did I tell you to run?"

"No," gasped Presto, doubled over, "but... Polka!"

"Yes, yes, alright." Her tone softened as she turned to Peri and opened the box.

There, nestled amongst odd buttons, scraps of lace and hooks and eyes, sat an exquisite pink and lilac shimmering shell.

"That's it!" Peri picked it up. "The Olani gave me this the last time I was in Ondine!"

"Good, now remember what I told you to do?"

"Yes, Forlana."

"Right, come on then - let's go!"

She led Peri towards the doors... to find Shawm and Dal blocking their path.

Forlana looked up from the barrel as she withdrew a mask and tank, frowning.

"Out the way, lads - we need to get going!"

"Peri, yes. But not _you_, Forlana."

"Of course I'm going - I'm her Mentor!"

Shawm shook his head.

"That's as maybe, but the Maestro left _you_ in charge. We can't risk you!"

Forlana looked livid.

Peri hastily went to fetch her underwater equipment.

"Don't be ridiculous," began Forlana, ready for a right royal row, when she was interrupted.

"He's right. You know he is!"

Forlana whirled round.

"And who asked _you_?"

"We don't have time to argue." Presto squared up to her, his eyes blazing. "Doesn't matter _who_ goes with Peri, as long as she comes back with that plant... for _Polka_!" He stressed the name, and it had the desired effect.

"Polka," repeated Forlana, looking at Presto, with tears in her eyes.

"We'll be back before you know it!" Presto grinned at her, grabbing the mask and tank out of her hands.

"Is this dragon of yours safe, Peri?"

Peri nodded, her helmet already in place, as Dash had signaled the dragon from the rear window to go round to the front once more.

Presto grabbed a couple of sacks, and made sure Peri had the shell safely, then he saluted Forlana.

Faye came to stand with her as they watched their two friends disappear into the mist.

"For Polka," whispered Faye, squeezing Forlana's arm.

Forlana nodded, as a tear rolled down her cheek.

"For Polka."

CHAPTER 8

At Scores Hall , there was a hive of activity such as had never been seen before.

Miss Scrivens had been very busy, compiling lists of what children played which instruments, then she totted them all up, and went to ask the Maestro what she should do next.

"Give them to Timp," Monody said wearily, "he can organise groups of students to dig out what we need, without making a drama of it." (He was, of course, thinking of Professor Cloche, who would have complained bitterly about being given such a mundane task)

"Are you alright, Maestro?" Miss Scrivens asked, worriedly. Over the past three or four days, she knew he'd had little, if any, sleep… and for the first time since she'd met him, a very long time ago, he was beginning to show his age.

He smiled and patted her hand.

"I'm fine, honestly."

She threw him a doubtful look, but left to carry out his bidding, waving a hand in acknowledgement as he called after her, "Don't forget about the Sotto Voce mats!"

He turned to see Fanfare coming towards him from the opposite corridor.

"How is everyone?" (By everyone, Fanfare knew he meant the magical creatures, not the Fairies.)

"The Sprites are improving, slowly; the bluebirds are eating normally again and even Brand is showing some small signs of improvement!"

The two old friends sighed in unison.

For a Beamer to attempt to fly through the Woodwind was incredible enough, for him to <u>succeed</u>, was truly amazing.

Monody marvelled anew at the intense bond that formed between Creature and Fairy, sometimes. (Or Creature and Human, come to that… look at Brio and Faye!)

He gave himself a small shake, in order to turn back to more pressing matters.

"I've put Timp in charge of locating all the instruments."

"A very good choice, Maestro. He will get it done quietly and efficiently."

Monody smiled.

"Indeed, more so than others, maybe?"

Fanfare smiled back, aware of whom the master was thinking.

"May I ask you a question, Maestro?"

"Of course, anything."

"These instruments are all going to Cadence Falls?"

"Correct."

"As are <u>all</u> the children?"

"Correct, again."

"Well, then... How are they going to play in the mist? Oh, I suppose the strings and percussion sections could manage well enough in masks, but the brass and the woodwind... oh!" He suddenly realised his unintended pun, but to his relief, the Maestro laughed heartily.

"I know, Fanfare! Using the woodwind section to destroy the Woodwind!"

Fanfare joined in, and as Monody wiped his eyes, he said, "Thank you old friend - I needed a good laugh - it chases the blues away!"

Fanfare nodded.

"Now, don't you worry about them playing <u>outside</u>, I have it all under control... if the dragons are willing!"

"The dragons!" Fanfare cried in dismay. "<u>That's</u> what I came to tell you! They're all assembled in the courtyard, waiting for your instructions!"

"Good!" The Maestro gripped his herald's arm. "It <u>will</u> be alright, Fanfare - you'll see!"

He strode off to get a mask and tank, before signaling for the huge harp-shaped door to be opened.

Fanfare watched him go, sighed and went to check that all the children had eaten a good meal. He stood on the small platform, looked around and said, "Shhh! Quiet, please!"

Unfortunately, he didn't possess his master's huge, resonating voice, and all but a few carried on talking.

Scott, however, had spotted him, and <u>he</u> had no problem in making himself heard.

"Can everybody be quiet!" he yelled.

Every face turned to look at him.

"I think they're trying to tell us something!"

He pointed at Fanfare, and all the children gave him their attention.

"Yes, hello. Yes, um... I just wanted to tell you that we'll be leaving for Cadence Falls soon. All the instruments have gone on ahead and will be waiting for you when you arrive."

"<u>How</u> have they 'gone ahead'? Did they fly?" Scott looked smugly at Fanfare, and the little herald felt a slight enjoyable stab of sarcasm as he replied, "Yes, they did. And so will you, shortly!"

Monody walked in just then to total chaos.

He raised his eyebrows questioningly, to which Fanfare replied, "I'm sorry, Maestro, but that <u>boy</u>!..."

Seeing the Composition Magician staring at him with those piercing eyes, Scott sat down quickly, and was quiet after that.

"My friends..." Strange how the Maestro could utter just two words... and command complete silence. Fanfare was more than relieved not to have to quieten them again.

"I have just spoken to our 'method of transport' and they are very willing to accommodate us!"

A few children looked puzzled; some looked scared, others merely curious.

Monody let the tension build for a few seconds then, winking at Fanfare, said calmly, "Prepare yourselves for an exciting ride... on dragons!"

The place erupted.

Leaving poor Fanfare to cope as best he could, the Maestro went swiftly to speak to all the staff and students, who had assembled, as asked, in one of the larger rehearsal rooms.

"Thank you for waiting. Your expertise as singers and musicians is about to be tested as never before. Our very lives will depend on what we do today. All I ask of you is to be the very best you can be - I can ask no more. Are you with me?"

"Yes, Maestro!" A hundred voices cried at once.

Monody gazed at them all, proudly.

"Madame Leider, Professor Tamburo, could I ask you to organise the first group who will go on dragon-back, to Cadence Falls.?"

"Of course, Maestro."

Madame Leider came forward to receive the lists of who was to go in which group, and began to organise the students, while Professor Tamburo made his way to the hall (with three of the lists) to sort out the children.

Monody watched for a minute, then left, satisfied that they had everything well in hand.

CHAPTER 9

Climbing the final flight of stairs, Monody drew a deep breath, focusing his thoughts on how best to proceed with this situation.

He knocked twice on the door at the top of the stairs and heard a curt, "Come in!"

He opened the door slowly and went inside.

"You'll have to wait a minute - this is the tricky part, so be quiet!"

Amused, the Maestro stood patiently to one side, while Lee Van Clef, wearing the strange-looking magnifying glasses that had scared Faye when she first met him, into thinking he was some kind of bug-eyed monster, carefully lower the beautiful crystal he held between a pair of tiny pliers, into an exquisite necklace of silver and lapis lazuli, (a really gorgeous shade of blue/green). Once it was set in the centre of a tiny guitar, Lee carefully closed the claws over the stone which held it in place.

Monody realised he'd been holding his breath and sighed.

"You really are a master of your craft, Lee."

The Crystal Crafter looked up in surprise, pulling his goggles off as he did so.

"Maestro! This is a pleasant surprise! I thought you were one of those pesky students they're always sending up to see if this or that is ready!..." He suddenly realised that he'd told his master to be quiet!

"I apologise, Maestro, if I'd have known it was you..."

"That's quite alright, Lee. It's quite refreshing to be ordered about, once in a while."

Lee chuckled.

"Glad I could help. Now, what can I do for you, Maestro?"

Monody became serious at once and took a seat opposite Lee.

"I have some news for you, which may come as a bit of a shock."

"Is it.. it's not, is it? I thought, for a moment, earlier, that I could hear dragons… but with all the noise that goes on in this place, it's a wonder anyone ever learns anything!"

He looked hopefully at the Composition Magician.

Sighing at the delay of the inevitable, Monody summoned up a smile.

"You <u>did</u> hear dragons, Lee - they're back!"

It was no wonder that Lee was both amazed and excited… and wanted to hear the whole story, but Monody felt that if he didn't tell Lee the reason he was there, soon, he would lose his nerve.

"Lee!" he cut across the other's questions.

"I will tell you how it all came about, later, I promise, but first, I <u>must</u> explain what has brought me up here!"

Something in his master's voice made Lee pause, mid-question, and stare at him.

Monody put his fingertips together and began quietly.

"A few days ago, Dal and the boys found a stranger, collapsed just by the Bar Barrier at Cadence Falls. They took him to the Warehouse nearby, where Fretta and Forlana took care of him. He was in a bad way and unconscious at first. He'd had a very serious injury to his leg and, we think, his head, some time ago… possibly in a rockslide." He paused, as he saw Lee suddenly clench his hands together until the knuckles turned white.

"When he finally came to," continued Monody, "it was obvious that he's been through some great hardships to survive," here, he looked up at Lee, "including being held captive in Dee Sharp's castle."

"No!" The word was wrenched from Lee's lips, as he turned pale.

"He <u>is</u> improving, daily, but the slightest excitement scares him, and sends him back into his shell. We've had to go <u>very</u> slowly with him. In fact, at first, the only way we could communicate with him at all was by asking him about his one possession - the thing that means more than the world to him… his oboe!"

Lee began to sob.

"I've heard him play, Lee. He hasn't lost one ounce of his considerable ability. In fact, it was his virtuoso playing which confirmed his identity."

He took the other Fairies hand in his.

"It <u>is</u> Dale, Lee. We've found him, at last."

Lee finally raised red, tear-stained eyes to the Maestro's.

"I must go to him now! If the dragons are back…"

He made to rise, but Monody held him down.

"You <u>shall</u> see him, soon, I promise, but I <u>must</u> make you understand, he's not the same… he doesn't remember."

"He'll remember _me_!" Lee said, angrily.

He was unprepared for Monody's sorrowful shake of the head.

"I'm sorry, Lee, but he doesn't. I mentioned earlier that we think he may have sustained a head injury during the rockslide that separated you, all those years ago. Fretta noticed some old scarring on one side of his head, when he first came in, and he's obviously had a bad leg injury at some point, because now he walks with a limp."

Lee nodded, trying desperately to take all this in.

"Fretta thinks that the head injury may have damaged his memory. His speech is slower than it was, and yet… his playing… he has forgotten none of that!"

"But how am I going to get him to remember _me_?" asked Lee in despair.

"Now, listen," the Maestro continued, gently. "Do you remember Faye, the girl who found her way up here on the day of the circus?"

"Faye? Yes, of course!"

"Well, she is on her way to Cadence Falls. I've instructed her to have a chat with Dale, and very casually, to drop the word 'brother' into the conversation. It may take some time for him to make the connection, but I think it could, eventually do the trick. You'll have to be patient with him, Lee. Faye will do her best and if anyone can get through to him, it'll be her. You'll come on the final dragon-trip to Cadence Falls, with me… and Lee… bring your violin."

"My violin?" Lee was confused. "Maestro, you know I haven't played since the day Dale disappeared."

"I know, but I need _every_ musician I can lay my hands on. Faye will lead us, when the time comes."

"Faye!" Lee looked at his master. "I knew there was something special about her!"

"There certainly is," replied the Maestro.

"She is the key!"

CHAPTER 10

"Okay. Are you sure you know what to do? Good! Once you've got it, we fly straight to the Red Barn, and then back to Cadence Falls, before Forlana has time to convince herself that it's all gone wrong without her!"

Presto gave her a comical look.

Peri laughed.

They were standing by the Pizzicato Pool, yelling at each other through their masks.

A large, purple dragon was curled up nearby, unconcernedly blowing clouds of the Woodwind away from them by snorting mightily.

She gave Presto a thumbs up.

"Have you got the shell?" He yelled at her.

Peri nodded, opening her palm so he could see the Sospiro Shell, nestling there.

"I'll be here when you get back… waiting!" he shouted, passing her the two sacks.

She smiled and watched him step back out of the way, laughing as a large foreleg suddenly shot out of the mist, scooped him up and plonked him down near the belly of the dragon, where the Woodwind wasn't so heavy.

His surprised expression was the last thing she saw before diving neatly into the pool and disappearing beneath the waters.

The two sacks, which she tied around her waist, weighed her down slightly as they filled with water, but she wasn't bothered, as she needed to swim to the bottom, anyway.

Suddenly, two Ondulandi appeared, seemingly out of nowhere, and swam in front of her, blocking her path.

Peri wasn't afraid for Forlana had told her to expect this.

She held out her right hand and opened it.

The Ondulandi looked at the Sospiro Shell, then at Peri, then one of them bowed, and beckoned her forward.

She swam after him, knowing their destination, and sure enough, after a while the beautiful city of Ondine came in sight, and Peri was led to the entrance of the same tower she had been to on her first visit.

Her guide then bowed and left her, to return to his friend farther up and resume their patrol.

Peri waited till he'd left, then turned and opened the little door that led inside the tower.

As if on cue, as she entered the tower, the opposite door opened, and the very same Ondulandi that Peri had met last time, appeared again!

This time, of course, Peri knew what was going to happen; the Water Sprite pressed several shells on the wall, and suddenly, all the water in the tower began to drain away. As soon as the level was lower than her head, Peri took off her helmet and, as before, a peg suddenly appeared in the wall for her to hang it on.

She then removed the tank and hung it up, before turning to the Ondulandi, with the water now splashing around her legs as it went, and bowed low.

"Greetings to the Ondulandi from the Music Fairies. Peri, their emis essi..." Here Peri stumbled a bit, before finally remembering the word Forlana had used.

"Peri, their emissary, humbly begs an audience with the new Olani, on a matter of great urgency." Peri sighed. She hoped she'd got it right.

"Can't I just tell them Polka needs help?" She'd said to Forlana, earlier.

"No! <u>You</u> know how formal and polite the Ondulandi are, Peri - you've met them before! You can't just go barging in saying "I want!"

"I suppose not," sighed Peri; as Forlana made her rehearse the first of her two speeches again and again.

Well, she'd done it - now what?

She realised the Ondulandi was waiting for something else... the bow! She'd forgotten to bow at the end of the speech. Peri hastily bowed low again and got another bow in response.

The Water Sprite disappeared back through the series of doors that led to the Olani's apartments.

Peri sighed. She hoped she wasn't going to have all the trials and tests she'd had to go through last time, before she could, at last, <u>speak</u> to the Olani!

They simply didn't have time, now, besides, she was worried about leaving Presto on the bank, out in the Woodwind. Even though he had a mask, she didn't think it was a good idea to just stand about in it!

The door suddenly opened, and to Peri's amazement, the new Olani came in to meet <u>her</u>! (Peri knew this by her robes and crown.)

Peri bowed very low, and as she rose, opened her palm once more, to display the Sospiro Shell.

She began her second speech.

"Oh, great and powerful Olani, I bring greetings from…" when suddenly the Olani held up her hand, silencing Peri in mid-sentence.

'Oh, no! What did I do wrong?' she thought. If she failed to get the Diapason Plant for Polka…

"Sit, please." The kind and calm voice of the Olani surprised Peri so much that she plonked herself down right where she stood.

"It is Peri?" The Olani smiled at her.

"Yes," Peri nodded, bowing her head.

"Only a great need would bring Peri to us through the green mist… what is this need?"

Only too happy to dispense with all the formalities, Peri explained how they needed more of the Diapason Plant which grew near the cave where the Tuna had lived.

The Olani nodded.

"Peri is good. Peri help Ondulandi to be free from Tuna, once more."

Peri nodded.

"Now, we help Peri. Go! Take many plants for Music Fairies. For Maestro - friends."

Peri sprang up. "Oh, thank you, thank you very much! I'm really grateful."

Peri was so relieved that she spoke so quickly that the Olani couldn't follow her.

Peri made herself say, "Thank you, oh great and powerful Olani," as clearly as she could, and followed it up with a couple of bows for good measure.

The Olani smiled and inclined her head in return, before opening the door and leaving.

Peri stood very still until the Olani was out of sight, then made a grab for her helmet and tank as her guide came back in.

"I take you to cave, Peri?"

"Yes, please. The Olani said I can gather as many Diapason Plants as I need for the Music Fairies!"

Her friend nodded, having obviously been told this by the Olani as she left.

Peri, clad once more in helmet and tank, waited for the tower to fill with water again and then her guide led her out into the waters and down the long twisting passages to what had been the Tuna's lair.

This time, of course, she didn't have to persuade him to let her have the plant, so they were able to swim through the opening at the back of the cave and out into what would have been, on dry land, a whole field of Diapason Plants!

Peri smiled at her guide, and between them they filled Peri's sacks up with the powerful plant.

As they swam away from Ondine and up towards the surface once more, the two guards intercepted them and offered to take the sacks. Peri waved her thanks to the guide, and the guards escorted her all the way back to just beneath the surface. There, they handed her the sacks, saluted, and dived back down again.

Peri pulled the heavy sacks up the last few feet and surfaced in the thick swirling mist, once more.

However, Presto and the dragon had moved to the edge of the pool, so strong hands were there to take the sacks and tie them tight against the Woodwind, whilst a helpful foreleg scooped her out of the water, and soon, Peri and Presto were a-dragonback, speeding towards the Red Barn… and Polka.

CHAPTER 11

Rollo was just crossing the main hall, carrying a huge pile of clean washing which Viola had given him, saying "This should keep your team supplied for a while," when a huge trumpeting noise made him drop the lot!

Scales, who had been dozing in his corner, sprang awake, crying, "Dragons!"

"Can't be!" replied Rollo, rushing with others to open the huge barn doors.

However, the doors were suddenly pushed open by a massive foreleg, and several Fairies, picking themselves up from the floor, were privileged to see, at close quarters, a huge purple dragon stroll into the barn as if it were the most normal thing in the world!

For a second, nobody moved, then Viola, gathering her wits, yelled "Door!" and everyone sprang into action.

Four Fairies ran to get the leaf fans used to shoo the mist out, and Scales dipped past his much larger cousin to help close the door.

The big dragon turned and watched with interest as Scales put his forelegs against the massive doors and they swung shut.

Only then, did anyone think to see who was riding the dragon.

"Presto! Peri!" cried Rollo joyfully, as they removed their helmets and masks... then he had to skip out of the way as a huge foreleg raised itself so that the passengers could clamber down.

Presto and Peri rushed to Rollo and Viola.

"Where's Polka? We've brought Diapason Plants - lots of them!"

"This way, quickly!"

They followed Viola to the Infirmary and there, a dreadful sight met their eyes.

Polka lay, totally still, not moaning nor moving... but still... like a statue.

Landler, barely recognisable, with dark circles under his eyes and sorrowful lines etched on his face, sat next to her, and, as he looked up at his friends, Peri thought she'd never seen anyone look so desolate in her life.

Presto, doing his best not to look shocked, went to kneel by his friend.

"Landler, we've brought the Diapason Plant for Polka. She'll improve, now, you'll see."

Landler shook his head slowly.

"She won't wake up."

Presto motioned the others out, behind his back, and the girls left him to it.

"Let me just give this to Corona and Canto, then we can talk," Viola said to Peri.

She rushed off to find the two Fairy Medics and Peri went back into the main barn. Quite a sight met her eyes.

Scales had invited his new friend to go and sit in the corner with him for an introductory chat, but the large dragons act of sitting had reverberated all the way round the room, and several Fairies were busy, clearing up broken crockery, cakes, pots of jam, and anything else that had been tumbled to the floor!

Those who weren't engaged in the clean-up stood staring, open-mouthed at the huge beast, who only just fitted in their massive barn, and who was taking no notice of the Fairies at all.

Rollo managed to tear his eyes away and went to Peri saying simply, "How?"

"The Draconis Stone was found by Scales, so the Maestro has been able to call the dragon's back!"

Rollo blinked a bit.

"<u>All</u> of them?"

"Yes," Peri smiled, "and, the best thing is that, like Scales, they're totally unaffected by the Woodwind, so we can use them as transport!"

Rollo went weak at the knees and had to sit down.

"So... so there really is some hope... at last?"

"Yes, Rollo. The Maestro has come up with an amazing plan; which I'm sure will work if we all pull together."

"What is it?"

"He hasn't told us all of it yet. All I know is, more dragons will be coming to take everyone to Cadence Falls, which is where everything will happen. Oh... and you're <u>all</u> to bring any instruments you play with you!"

Rollo blinked again, but was too dazed to speak, so it was just as well that Viola returned at that moment.

She sat down at their table and looked at Peri.

"Corona has made the mixture containing the Diapason Plant in record time, and we have given Polka her first dose, but it is far too soon to tell if it's working yet. Corona is also worried that the juice from the plant has not had time to settle yet before being used, so they are making another batch, which can be left to stand overnight, in case the first one isn't strong enough."

"But she looks so terrible!" Peri blurted out, before she could stop herself.

Viola took her hand and patted it.

"I know it seems very bleak, but I've known Polka since we were younglings, and although she may be gentle in her ways, she has a very determined streak in her nature! She <u>knows</u> how much Landler needs her, and that will make her fight - I'm certain of it!"

Peri wiped away her tears, and then realised she was using the handkerchief that Polka had made for her and swallowed hard.

"If you're certain of it, Viola, then so am I!"

"That's the spirit, Peri," said Rollo, getting up as he saw Presto coming towards them.

"How is she?" they all asked at once.

Presto nodded.

"She's had the medicine and Corona is sitting in with Landler to wait for any signs of improvement."

"How's <u>he</u> doing, now?" enquired Rollo.

"Slightly better... now there's hope."

They all sighed.

Presto shook his head.

"He didn't even realise Brio had left for Cadence Falls!"

"Oh, thank goodness! <u>That's</u> where he went! Is he alright?"! clamoured Viola and Rollo together.

"You mean, no one knew where he'd gone?" cried Peri in alarm.

"No!" Rollo replied. "He wasn't missed till the following morning, as we all assumed he'd gone to his quarters, after his chat with scales. I did wonder about him maybe trying to connect, somehow, with Forlana, (we didn't know if you and Faye had returned, at that point) But I never dreamed he'd actually <u>fly</u> there <u>on</u> <u>his</u> <u>own</u>!"

He's very weak, but alive." said Presto.

"He's the most extraordinary Beamer I've ever known," said Viola, dabbing at her eyes.

"We ought to be getting on, Peri... are you ready to leave?"

"Yes, of course," Peri said, jumping up. "I'll just go and see if our ride has finished his chat."

She crossed over to where Scales and the large dragon were in deep conversation.

"Peri!" cried Scales. "This is Accelerando. He's just been telling me that there are loads more dragons now, back at Scores Hall, and they're <u>all</u> going to help the Maestro defeat Dee Sharp! Isn't that good? I can't wait to meet them all!"

Peri smiled and patted his nose.

"Does this mean that you'll be leaving now, Scales?"

The little dragon looked up at the big one, his eyes shining with excitement, but then, he lowered his head and looked at Peri, once more.

"I need to stay here, Peri," he said, quietly. "Landler may need me to take him to the Maestro, once Polka is better… so I'll stay."

Peri gave him a great big hug.

"You may not be the biggest," she whispered to him, "but you're the best and bravest dragon I know!"

CHAPTER 12

Monody walked down to the main hall, consulting the lists in his hand as he did so. The first 'wave' of children, students and teachers had already left for Cadence Falls and he was just about to call out the names of the next wave, and get them assembled, ready to leave.

He paused just outside the doors to catch his breath before striding in to make the next announcement.

Monody had his hand out to pull the door open, when he heard an unmistakable tread behind him. Turning round he saw Fanfare, a troubled look on his face, approaching.

Swallowing a sigh for whatever new headache was about to come his way, the Composition Magician managed a smile.

"Fanfare, what can I do for you?"

"Could I have a quick word with you in the study?"

Fanfare didn't stress the word 'study', so Monody knew he meant his study, not the one where the Circle of Five met.

The Maestro's study wasn't far from the hall, so they reached it quickly and as soon as he closed the door, Fanfare said, "We've had a warning!"

Monody frowned for a moment, then understood.

"From the Tuna…?"

Fanfare nodded, grimly.

When the Maestro had rescued a large Tuna, who was accidentally imprisoned at the bottom of the Pizzicato Pool, where the Ondulandi lived, the Tuna, in gratitude for his release, had offered to give the Fairies due warning if it saw large numbers of angry Dots flying towards the Waterfall by the edge of the Seas of Man, for this could only mean one thing…

"A Deluge?" Monody's voice begged Fanfare to contradict him.

"I'm afraid so," the herald replied, worriedly. "What can we do?"

A Deluge was a dreadful thing to have to fight in the best of circumstances, but the thought of his people out in that lethal Woodwind, trying to capture all those discarded Dots before Dee

Sharp could call them to her, made him shudder.

The Composition Magician was silent for a moment, but Fanfare knew him well enough to realise he was thinking fast.

"Right!" He handed Fanfare the lists he had been carrying. "You're in charge, overall. Madame Leider will look after the remaining children. I'll send word with one of the dragons, once it's safe for the next wave to come. I must go."

He gripped Fanfare's arm in farewell and disappeared out into the corridor.

"Be safe," he whispered to the empty air, then blinked, took a deep breath, and went to find Madame Leider.

Monody, meanwhile, went round gathering Tamburo, Cloche and Lee Van Clef.

"There's a Deluge at Cadence Falls - we need to leave now! Tamburo, round up the Basses!" was all he said, but the other's obeyed without question, even the irritable Professor Cloche.

Soon, four large dragons, their wings swirling the green mist away from their passengers, flew steadily in the direction of Cadence Falls.

The Maestro had Lee behind him, and four of the Basses on one dragon, while Tamburo and Cloche (who was clinging on for dear life) and another four Basses were astride the other. Two more dragons carried the rest.

None of the Fairies had any idea where they were, for the Woodwind had obscured everything from view, but the dragons knew… and that was good enough for Monody.

When, at last, they reached Cadence Falls, a scene of chaos met their eyes!

All the Music Fairies and Gnomes were busy, trying to fight the Deluge in the Woodwind whilst wearing masks, so they couldn't speak clearly to each other.

The Team of Fairies clambered down the dragons as best they could, and immediately, as their passengers were on the ground, the four dragons took flight, which had the effect of clearing a lot of the Woodwind out of the way.

Monody knew a seconds panic - why were the dragons leaving so suddenly?

But then he saw - they were only going as far as the Bar Barrier; there to turn the Dots back, away from the Cacophony Wood, and Dee Sharp!

The Fairy folk saw this, and Monody could tell that they were cheering, by the fists being pumped in the air, although he couldn't hear them.

All the new-comers took the opportunity of seeing, temporarily, where they were, to move forward and grab pails and shovels and anything else they could find.

They worked hard alongside the others, but it seemed for every barrow-load the Gnomes wheeled round to the Warehouse, as many Dots came cascading over the Waterfall to taunt them.

Catch and Glee were both wheeling their seventh barrow-load into the Warehouse, where Shawm and Dal were organising a group of Gnomes to barrel up the Dots and seal the lids, and store them in the corner where Crumhorn and Dash were making sure they were stacked securely.

Catch looked up at one of the stacks, thinking it was too high; they normally never stacked more than five barrels on top of each other, but today, everyone was rushing, trying to deal with the unusual number of discarded Dots so that these stacks were almost double in height.

Catch went to take his mask off, intending to tell Shawm that a stack that high could be dangerous, when, to his horror, one of the stacks suddenly leaned over and collapsed!

Dash looked up from his position underneath the barrels - he'd never get out in time!

When suddenly, he was pushed violently to one side and fell, rolling away from the falling barrels that landed with a huge crash, right where he had been standing.

One barrel had burst, so the next few minutes were spent in scooping all the Dots up into a new one, and when this was finally done, Dash said with a relieved grin, "That was a close one, eh, Crumhorn?"

He turned around, looking for his friend, and then saw the small group of Gnomes clustered around the fallen barrels.

Dash made his way over to them, saying, "What's up, lads? Anyone seen Crumhorn?"

And then he stopped… for there, lying in between bits of broken wood and battered metal hoops, lay Crumhorn, green blood oozing from his head and side.

Dash knelt down and took his hand. His eyes slowly fluttered open.

"Good," the Goblin said, slowly, "I did save you!"

"You pushed me out the way of the barrels?" Dash said in

amazement.

"Yes." The voice was fainter now.

"You and Lilt - you changed our lives. Tell Sackbut to <u>always</u> live like a Gnome. Look after him... Dash?"

And he was gone...

Gnomes return to the earth from whence they came; Fairies become part of the ether, but when a Goblin dies, he turns into rocks and stones.

Shawm went to fetch Sackbut and Lilt, and they, together with Dash, gently removed the boulders that had once been crumhorn and laid them carefully to one side.

Lilt took a dazed Sackbut back to the barrel of masks and tanks.

"We'll honour him right, later, after we've dealt with all this. He's a hero, Sackbut - never forget that - he saved Dash's life!"

Sackbut nodded as a tear rolled down his cheek.

Dash came over and gripped his arm.

"I owe Crumhorn my life. The last thing he said... was for you. 'Always live like a Gnome'... So we must work together to win this battle, yes?"

Crumhorn nodded and picked up a mask.

"We work to save Cadence Falls... together!"

CHAPTER 13

Landler quietly strummed on his guitar, making sure it was in tune.

During his brief visit, Presto had told him that playing music to Faires affected by the Woodwind had proved very beneficial.

A group of Gnomes or Fairies went up to the Treatment Centre every day to play for them and Fretta had reported a decided improvement in their condition.

Well, if it had worked in Cadence Falls, perhaps it would work here. Landler would give anything a try!

Polka had now been given her fourth dose of the Diapason Plant concoction and Corona, when she had come in to check on Polka, had told him that now it was just a case of 'wait and see'.

Landler ran his fingers up a G chord and began to play - a simple folk tune that he didn't have to concentrate on, so he could think!

So much had happened in such a short space of time, that it made him dizzy.

First of all, Presto had informed him that he reached Faye, telepathically, all the way over to Scores Hall! Landler had no idea how he'd achieved that! It was just that his need to tell her of the Diapason Plant had been so great!

Then there had been the astonishing behaviour of the Beamers. Brand had flown to Scores Halls, to inform him that Polka was sick, and then, apparently, Brio had flown, half-blind and unaided to Cadence Falls to let them know that Polka needed to be treated with the Diapason Plant.

Landler had always had admiration for his Beamer friends, but until now, had no idea of the true love and loyalty that the butterflies gave to those with whom they chose to form a bond!

To his shame, he hadn't even noticed that Brio had left that day - he was so wrapped up in Polka that nothing else seemed to matter!

His thoughts went back to Faye. In all his studies (and he'd done a lot) on Human children and their Fairy mentors, he'd never come across a telepathic link before, and yet this had happened <u>twice</u> with Faye, now! Once when she'd been injured in a fall in the Cacophony Wood, and then now, while Polka was so sick.

He'd spoken of it to the Maestro, who'd told him in his calm way, that though it wasn't impossible, it was certainly unusual for a Fairy to have such a strong mind-link to a Human.

But Landler <u>knew</u> Faye was special - he'd known it that day when she'd 'felt' that something was wrong at the Falls. She was very young to have such power and he was constantly afraid she'd overtax herself in her determination to help the Music Fairies. Indeed, she'd nearly died, the time she'd stayed too long in Octavia, and <u>that's</u> when they discovered all about the Diapason Plant!

Without even realising it, Landler had changed his gentle strumming to play the love song that Polka had been singing the night he realised he loved her! Polka… everything led back to her. The Diapason Plant that his friends had risked so much to bring for her. The song he was playing… it all led to her.

He began to hum the vocal line, very gently, while tears rolled down his cheeks (he was far too emotional to be able to sing it) and he heaved a shuddering sigh.

A sudden movement made him stop humming. A fluttering hand brushed against his arm, as if seeking reassurance that he was there.

Landler dared to look down at the tiny hand and took it carefully in his own.

"Dearest?" The voice was barely a whisper, but the tone was one he'd not dared to hope for.

"Polka?"

He turned to look at her, just as her eyes fluttered open to reveal a puzzled expression.

"Why am I in bed?"

Landler blinked.

"Dearest, you really shouldn't be sitting around here when there's so much to do!" she reprimanded him, softly.

He smiled through his tears at her.

"Oh, my Polka!" He gathered her into his arms and hugged her as tightly as he dared.

"Landler! she laughed, shakily, "suppose someone comes in!"

"Let them!" He kissed her soundly and she blushed.

"Landler, really! What's got into you? I can't lie about here -

there's work to be done!"

She made as if to rise, but he placed a restraining hand on her shoulder.

"Polka, dearest… the fact is, you haven't been very well. I don't know how much you remember…?"

"We were at Pavane Villa, weren't we? I remember we went there <u>suddenly</u> when we'd planned to go to Galliard…?"

"That's right. But the Maestro sent us to <u>his</u> place, because he thought we'd be safe there…" he trailed off.

Polka frowned, trying to remember.

"It was the Woodwind, dearest. Rollo and Presto came to rescue us, but you'd already inhaled some of the mist, by then, and well… it made you ill."

She stared at him, then looked around, finally realising where they were.

"We're at the Red Barn!"

"Yes - the Beamers flew us here through the Woodwind, because it was closest. Do you remember?"

She shook her head.

"You just had a cough, at first, so I… I went to deliver the masks that Rollo had made, and I was at Scores Hall when you became really ill."

"So… how did you know?" she asked, puzzled.

He swallowed hard.

"Brand flew on his own, to Scores Hall to tell me, and <u>then</u> once we realised you needed the Diapason Plant, Brio also flew, <u>without a guide</u>, to let Forlana, Faye and Peri know. Presto and Peri went to the Pizzicato Pool, and she dived to get it for you and, well… now you're better."

"They did all that… for <u>me</u>?" She raised incredulous eyes to his.

"They love you, you see… as do I!" He flashed his brilliant smile at her; the one that made her heart skip a beat every time she saw it.

"Well, but… dearest… shouldn't you be <u>doing something</u> to help in this crisis?"

He laughed; a laugh of sheer relief - his old Polka was back!

"I <u>should</u> be doing several things, of course, but none of them as important as making sure <u>you're</u> alright!"

"I'm fine, dearest really!"

"Hmm, we'll see. You'll stay there until the Medics have looked at you; I won't be far away."

She laughed at him.

"Go on! I can see you're itching to get busy again!"

He kissed the top of her head as he got up to leave.

"You do <u>know</u> I love you, Polka, don't you?"
"Of course I do," she smiled. "Just as much as I love you."

Landler left the room whistling a happy little tune that he hadn't dared to think about while his world seemed to be crashing about his ears. He hadn't sung it in ages, but now, despite all the perils and hardships they had yet to face, it seemed to suit his mood.

CHAPTER 14

By the evening, a large group of exhausted Music Fairies, Gnomes and children, sat trying to eat the delicious stew that Ocarina had prepared, but to be honest, no one really had an appetite.

The Deluge had finally been brought under control, but without the dragon's help, Monody didn't think they'd have had a chance… and then there was Crumhorn.

As soon as everyone was seated, the Maestro had gone round from table to table, mixing just the right amount of sympathy in his voice with the positive message that now was <u>not</u> the time to let sadness overtake them, as they had the biggest battle yet to come over the next two days and they <u>all</u> needed to be at their best.

We'll show Crumhorn the proper respect he deserves, once the danger is past, but for <u>now</u>, we must focus on what's to be done!"

Monody went back to his table, and some much-needed food, aware, from the bits and pieces of conversation he could overhear, that most of the Gnomes genuinely regretted Crumhorn's passing.

A few people were glancing over to where the first wave of children to arrive, sat in a miserable huddle with Faye and Peri.

Monody felt sorry for them: they'd been hauled out of their world, not to their usual Mezzo Meadow, (there were, in fact, several of these, dotted around Octavia) where their own Mentor would be waiting for them, but to a strange hall that most of them had never <u>seen</u> before, told that they were all to be part of a master plan… then thrown on the back of a <u>very</u> large dragon, flown who knows where through a thick, green mist, only to be pushed into a warehouse, once they arrived, because the air was thick with angry, swarming black things!

Faye and Peri had been doing a marvellous job of calming them all down, thought Monody. He'd literally thrust the girls into the role of 'minders' as soon as he'd arrived at the Warehouse.

"Look after them, will you? You know what's going on... they don't."

Faye and Peri, who were by now used to obeying orders said, "Of course, Maestro," and began to usher the frightened children in, taking their masks and oxy-tanks from them and handing out drinks.

Monody ate mechanically, wearily transferring his gaze to the curtained area, behind which, Lee had just gone to see his brother for the first time in years...

... Dale sat, oboe in hand, as always, with a bemused look on his face. As he had been instructed, Lee had entered quietly and asked about the instrument first, before saying, simply: "My name is Lee," and producing his violin (which he'd hastily strapped to his backpack when they'd suddenly had to leave!)

"Play him something from when you were both young," the Maestro had said. "Wait to see if he joins in with you; if he <u>does</u>, it's a good sign!"

Lee began to play a simple little folk tune that they had learned, years ago.

Dale listened for a minute or two, then placed his oboe to his lips and began to play... tentatively at first, but then cleverly weaving a harmony around the melody that Lee played.

They twisted and turned the music around between them, enjoying the first duet that they had shared in so very long.

As the tune rose merrily to it's close, Lee deliberately fluffed the last two bars, playing a run of notes in the wrong order.

As soon as they stopped, Dale said, "You never could play that last bit correctly! I remember <u>every</u> time you..."

He stopped, and slowly, <u>really</u> looked at Lee's face.

"Lee," he said, experimentally, then, "LEE??!"

Nodding happily, Lee stretched out a hand to clasp his brother's arm... Brothers, in truth, once more.

***

Back at the Red Barn, Landler and Rollo were busy organising the mass exodus that would take place when the dragons arrived, the following day.

As Presto and Peri, having delivered the Diapason Plant, were getting ready to leave, Presto had whispered, "That dragon just spoke to me! Told me to tell you that they'll be here in the morning. The Maestro has requested that you send people in two groups, according to how many masks and tanks are available to you; the dragons can do several trips, if need be!"

"We gave most of them away, Presto, as you know, but I'll check and see what's left... er... he's very efficient, isn't he?"

"Who? The Maestro?"

"No. I was thinking of <u>him</u>!" Rollo whispered, looking up at the huge beast who stood patiently by the Barn doors, waiting for Presto. (Peri had already clambered aboard.)

"Yes!" laughed Presto. "I suppose he is," ... and with that he'd put on his mask, and disappeared into the Woodwind with Peri, on their massive mount.

And now, Polka was on her way to recovery, which was marvellous, and Landler was back to his usual commanding self, thank goodness!

"Come on then, Rollo. If we tie all the brass instruments together with a couple of those nets that Corona found, we may be able to loop them across the dragons' shoulders, which will save space <u>and</u> time!"

"Good idea!" Rollo called after him, as the tall Fairy strode further into the barn in search of nets.

Rollo turned back to <u>his</u> task of making certain every mask and tank was properly joined together and in good working order.

They'd already made lists of who would go in each 'wave', much as the Maestro had done, in <u>his</u> turn, at Scores Hall.

The Red Barn, being a place of hard, physical work, it was lucky that they had no elderly or infirm Fairies, (In fact, Polka had been the only patient in the Infirmary!) and very <u>few</u> younglings. This made it easier to divide everyone up into four groups. Rollo wrote out a copy of each list and gave them to Viola, so she could let everyone know which group they would be in.

That done, he was just checking with Volta that every Fairies instrument had been brought into the main barn, (unless, like Volta's pipes, they were small enough to be carried on their person) when a voice by the door behind him made Rollo spin around.

"Hello, can I help?"

"Polka!" Rollo and Volta rushed over, one either side of the 'patient' and sat her gently down on a stool.

"Are you alright?" "Should you be up?" "Can I get you anything?" they both chorused, together.

Polka laughed.

"Yes, I'm fine; Canto and Corona have just proclaimed me fit to be up and about."

Rollo took her hand.

"Polka, we were all <u>so</u> worried… and, as for Landler…" Rollo swallowed hard as he remembered what his friend had endured.

"I'm so sorry to have caused you all so much worry and trouble," she said, in her gentle way.

"Not at all," cried Volta, squeezing her arm. "We're just happy to have you back and ready to come and do battle with us!"

"Er.. <u>are</u> you coming with us?" Rollo asked, tentatively. He could just imagine Landler's face if he thought, for one moment, the Polka was overtaxing herself!

"I've been told I can come," she smiled. "I'm a singer, not an instrumentalist, so all I need to do is to stand where I'm told, <u>when</u> I'm told, and sing!"

Volta smiled at Rollo.

"That's sorted, then."

By the evening all was ready, packed and prepared.

The entire workforce at the Red Barn had joined together for a hearty meal before a good night's sleep, which would bring them a new tomorrow… and the Maestro's plan!

CHAPTER 15

As Monody stirred and forced himself awake, he felt as though he'd barely had an hours sleep, which was probably close enough, as there had been dragons arriving with their passengers late into the night!

These were mostly from Scores Hall and, although the dragons seemed tireless, their passengers most certainly were not!

Fretta, Minima and Ocarina had done a splendid job of lining up make-shift pallets for those who needed to sleep, and serving stew to those who were hungry, and as soon as they'd done that, the next wave began to arrive, and they had to start the whole process all over again. (In fact, the Red Barn contingency had started to arrive just before dawn!)

The Warehouse, once seemingly so spacious, was packed to the rafters with drowsy Fairies, Gnomes and children!

Monody made his way to the little cloakroom off the side of the main room. He'd better get in there first, he thought, for who knew when there would be another chance!

It was, of course, built for Gnomes, so it was a bit of a squeeze for the Maestro, but he found it adequate for his needs, and came out rubbing a blue mint-stick across his teeth quickly. (Faye had found that these little sticks turned her teeth blue... they were meant for Fairies and Gnomes, not Humans! But fortunately, the effect wasn't permanent!)

The Warehouse was waking up in earnest now, so Monody picked up his pace and crossed to the food area. He was going to need a good breakfast. Ocarina obviously had the same thought, for she served him a large bowl of porridge, plus two thick slices of bread and a wedge of cheese!

"There's a pot of Lupin tea on your table, waiting for you, Maestro."

"Thank you, Ocarina!" He gave her a winning smile and made his way to the small table he shared with Forlana.

They made a quick breakfast, then Monody crossed to the little dais where the musicians had performed every evening since the Warehouse had become their temporary home and held up his hand for silence.

"Thank you, everyone!" he projected, taller than most people there, he loomed large on the small stage.

"Good morning! I hope you have all had a chance to get something to eat."

A general assent and clinking of spoons, gave him the answer.

"Good! It will not be long now before we are ready to leave. We are just waiting for the last few people to arrive and then we can… ah!"

He paused as he heard dragons trumpeting outside; the Gnomes on duty ran to heave open the doors and allow the last three groups of Fairies to arrive. The doors were hastily closed; the teams took off their masks and tanks and, as the last three people removed their gear, a massive cheer went up as the crowd saw Rollo, Landler… and Polka!

They started to chant her name: "Pol-ka! Pol-ka!"

Polka looked this way and that, not understanding, before she was almost knocked off her feet by Forlana, who came pelting through the crowd to get to her.

"Polka! Oh, Polka!" She squeezed her friend hard, then remembered she'd been ill, and let go quickly.

"Forlana," Polka smiled at her best friend, "why is there all this fuss? I've only been gone a few days?"

Forlana shook her head, crying with relief, (a thing she never did in public!) before turning to hug her brother.

Faye and Peri were next, seizing hold of her hands - both of them laughing and crying at the same time.

"Enough!" cried Polka, turning to the Maestro in embarrassed confusion.

"Everyone is delighted, my dear - that is all!"

He glanced meaningfully at Landler, who, at once, took Polka's arm and led her to a seat, away from the curious crowd.

"For those of you who don't know," the Maestro continued smoothly, "Polka is one of our most valuable Music Fairies. She has been very ill, but now, thankfully, she is better, and can join this fight today."

Another cheer went up, and poor Polka looked as though she

would rather be <u>under</u> the table than seated <u>at</u> it, but Landler beamed at her, and she stayed where she was.

"One more arrival and we can…"

The door moved a crack, and Dal rushed to pull it open, and then, in came Fanfare, swamped in a mask that was miles too big for him. He was also struggling with a large, heavy casket, that Lee and Dale quickly took from him and set it down between them.

Fanfare took his mask off, bowed to Monody and said, "Maestro, all is prepared."

"Excellent! <u>Now</u>, we move!"

"To <u>where</u>, Maestro?" asked Faye.

"We are going to prepare a line of defence along the Bar Barrier," said Monody. "You will discover your instruments waiting for you there. Once you arrive, please take off your masks and oxy-tanks, and the dragons will bring them back ready for the next group."

"But Maestro," Faye asked, "if we take them off <u>outside</u>, how will we be able to avoid breathing in the Woodwind?"

"You will see - <u>all</u> will become clear," smiled the Composition Magician.

He turned to look for Fanfare, who was busy shaking Dale's hand as if he would never stop, while Lee looked on smiling.

"Fanfare," the Maestro went to him, "plenty of time to catch up, <u>later</u>."

"I'm <u>so</u> sorry, Maestro!" Fanfare hastily turned back to his master and gave him several lists he had stored in his pocket.

"Right!" The Maestro went to the dais once more. "Would the following people please put a mask and tank on, ready to leave."

He called out thirty or so names, a mixture of Gnomes, Humans and Fairies. They all went to get ready, the Gnomes carrying smaller instruments, such as pennywhistles and flutes, with them. (The larger instruments had already been transported by the dragons earlier.)

As the first group left, Monody called 'his' team to him.

Fanfare, Landler, Polka, Forlana, Presto, Rollo, Faye and Peri all clustered round.

"You'll come last of all," he told them. "I have placed you all together in the centre, where you'll be strongest. Remember, just <u>feel</u> the music; let it flow <u>through</u> you, don't fight it. It'll feel strange, at first, but I'm relying on <u>all</u> of you to lead the others; they'll follow <u>you</u>!" He paused and looked at each of them in turn. "Thank you, my friends, let's hope that we're enough!"

"We <u>will</u> be!" Landler sounded so certain that the Maestro was filled with more hope than ever before!

CHAPTER 16

When Landler saw the penultimate group getting ready to leave (Forlana and Polka were handing out masks and oxy-tanks) he called Faye and Peri over.

"How are you both feeling?"

"Fine, Landler," replied Faye.

In truth, they were so excited by what was about to happen, that neither of them had given the Woodwind much thought.

As if sensing this, Landler looked at them, seriously.

"<u>Don't</u> underestimate the power of the Woodwind," he told them, sternly. "It's extremely strong, dark magic and, although the Maestro has put as many safeguards in place as he can, there is always the danger that it could sneak in during an unguarded moment. If you find you're doubting yourself, that'll be it! Don't let yourself have <u>any</u> negative thoughts, at all, for if you do, they will only get stronger as it tries to destroy you. Remember, concentrate on the music and the Maestro!"

The girls nodded solemnly, then Peri asked about something that had been puzzling her.

"Landler, we're going to be right in front of the Maestro, aren't we, so he can conduct us?"

"That's right," Landler nodded.

"But there are hundreds of Music Faires, Gnomes and kids, all stretched out along the Bar Barrier... how on earth are <u>they</u> all going to see him?"

"Did you notice the large casket that Fanfare brought in with him?"

"Yes!" cried Faye. "It looked to be much too heavy for him."

"But the Maestro would not have entrusted <u>anyone</u> other than Fanfare with it. You see, it holds the key which will enable this plan to work."

The girls looked at each other, then back at Landler.

"That's all I'm saying," was the only reply they got, as he moved away towards Presto, who had just called him over.

"What do you think he meant?" asked Peri.

Faye shrugged. Forlana was coming towards them now - perhaps she'd know. But Forlana was in 'organisation' mode and had no time to chat.

"Right, you two! Once those masks come back, it'll be our turn." She looked round.

"Rollo!" she beckoned him over, not wishing to shout her question.

"Is there enough oxy-thingy left inside the tanks to get us all there safely?"

"Ye...es," he said, lengthening the word, " ... just - They must be fairly close to empty, by now."

No one said it, but they were all thinking, if the Maestro's plan <u>didn't</u> work, they'd all be stranded out there, with no way of getting back to the Warehouse!

"Come on!" Forlana suddenly said, sharply, clapping her hands. "We all need to be <u>very</u> positive... this <u>is</u> going to work, as long as we all do what the Maestro said." She raised her voice, "So, come <u>on</u>, team!"

They all came round in a circle, together with the last few Fairies and Gnomes who would make up the final group. Everyone gripped each other's hands firmly.

"Let's all work together!" cried Forlana, and the resounding reply came back from everyone...

"TOGETHER!"

***

Faye looked around at all the folk she could see, knowing that the huge orchestra stretched much farther around the Bar Barrier than the eye could see in either direction.

As the Maestro had said, they were slap-bang in the middle, right in front of where the Composition Magician would stand; on a large podium, facing them all.

When they had arrived, the girls had been amazed to see a huge, lilac, shimmering dome, hovering over the hundreds of instruments that had been put out in readiness. A hotch-potch of seats, many of which Faye recognised from the Fairy Festival and the Handclasping, (how long ago both seemed now!) were placed in front of the Maestro and beyond, in semi-circular rows.

The Maestro indicated that Faye should take her place at the one and only piano she could see, (and which one of the very largest dragons must have brought from the Hall.)

Why did she, alone, have a piano? She could see several Fairies and some of the children on either side of her had Sotto Voce Mats unrolled on their laps. (Indeed, Faye had one hidden away in her bedroom at home, to practise on.)

Why hadn't she just been given one of those?

But there wasn't time to ponder over it, for Peri was whispering frantically to her, having found both flute <u>and</u> violin, next to her seat.

"What am I supposed to play first? I can't play both at once!"

Faye grinned at her and shrugged.

"Don't worry; I'm sure you'll know when to change over."

"I hope so!" said Peri, glancing round at the others.

Forlana had a small guitar and would also sing, Landler had <u>his</u> guitar, and Polka, with her splendid contralto voice, would simply sing.

Souza, over to her far left, was holding the large brass instrument he was named for, and Rollo, the girls knew, played a pennywhistle, as did many of the Gnomes, who were seated behind them.

Peri, who knew a little more about orchestra's than Faye, wondered why the Maestro hadn't arranged them all in sections - strings, woodwind, brass and percussion; the players were all dotted about, but Peri thought the Maestro, perhaps had a reason for doing it this way.

Faye suddenly waved at Scales, as she spotted him to her far right, sitting behind his drum kit. Some of the older dragons, the Maestro had told her, were very interested to discover that Scales could play; Faye wondered if any of <u>them</u> would discover a musical talent, once this battle was over.

She looked around for the other dragons, and suddenly saw that they were all stretched out, wing-tip to wing-tip, around the perimeter of the dome, behind her, and just inside of them, stood every Beamer Butterfly that they could muster, including, much to Faye's great relief, Brio and Brand.

All of the creatures seemed to be concentrating on something very hard indeed, and Faye wondered what it could be.

Brio, alerted to Faye's presence by the huge wave of relief she'd felt on seeing him, flashed her a very quick image of the dragons, the Beamers and Professors Tamburo and Cloche all focusing on the magic needed to keep the dome in place.

Magic! Was <u>that</u> the Maestro's secret weapon?

Forlana had told her the Music Fairies didn't use magic…

However, when, at that moment, the Maestro bent down and opened the heavy lid to the casket Fanfare had brought, Faye suddenly realised, as the Maestro raised his baton, exactly what his plan was to defeat Dee Sharp!

CHAPTER 17

The Maestro raised both arms, his hands held wide, and suddenly, out of the casket, floated strands of music, silver staves with the key signatures, dots, notes and rests, all written in black ink so that they were <u>very</u> clear and easy to read.

The music floated off to left and right, then, as it got far enough away from the centre, began to attach itself to… the Bar Barrier!

Of course! Thought Faye. The Bar Barrier was exactly that! She'd wondered why the black horizontal and vertical bard were placed in such a way, it had always reminded her of <u>something</u>… and suddenly, there it was! Empty bars, for music to be written on; they were filling up now, and, as they came to meet in the middle, the Maestro swept the silver baton that he held in his right hand, out across the orchestra.

Everyone stared at him, anxious not to miss a single instruction.

He raised his left-hand palm upwards, just slightly, and every singer stood up, as one, just as if they'd rehearsed it.

The Maestro pointed his baton at Fanfare, who at once, played an F on his violin. Everyone followed suit, and soon there was a huge F major chord, resounding out and along the whole dome, and now Faye could see the really clever part of this plan.

The music floated <u>out</u> of the top of the dome and hovered over the edge of the Cacophony Wood. So, the dome was magic, too! Nothing could get <u>in</u> but music could get <u>out</u>!!

Faye barely had time to realise this, when the Maestro swept his hands up, and as he brought them down, everyone, without knowing quite <u>how</u>, sprung into a bright, sprightly march; it was the sort of music you might hear if a military band was marching through the streets with people cheering.

Faye thought she might have heard it before, somewhere, but she could <u>never</u> have played it. Her sight-reading wasn't very good yet, (Peri's was much better,) but the beauty of it was her fingers seemed to have a life of their own!

Faye watched them, fascinated as they marched across the keys, just as the score of music marched and skipped along the Bar Barrier.

Faye felt a great surge of joy, which the Maestro seemed to sense for, while he was conducting, he suddenly glanced at her and nodded. They were repeating a section, at this point, that they'd already played, so Faye allowed herself a seconds lapse in concentration to watch the merry Dots dance their way <u>into</u> the Cacophony Wood. They didn't, as Faye had rather hoped, <u>beat</u> the Woodwind back, but cut their way through the mist, instead.

Faye hoped the merry, dancing Dots wouldn't end up becoming the dreaded Discords that she and Brio had fought so hard to destroy! It was only for a second, that she saw a mental picture of the Discords, but it was enough.

By now, the orchestra, without Faye having even realised it, had brought the march to a close. Without knowing how she did it, Faye's fingers picked up a little, lilting 6/8 melody and the rest of the orchestra followed suit.

Pleased at how well this all seemed to be going, Faye was totally unprepared for what happened next!

Suddenly, looming, looking out of the green mist, came a ravaged, evil face, right before her... a face that Faye hoped she'd never have to see again... Dee Sharp!

Faye's fingers missed a couple of notes, and she glanced up frantically at the Maestro. A slight frown was the only indication he gave that he knew Dee Sharp was there.

He smiled gently at Faye and nodded, so she, encouraged, kept going; looking at her hands, so she wouldn't have to look at the evil face which stared so hard at her, only a few feet away.

A sudden surge of power hit the dome. It wavered... but held fast. Peri and Faye exchanged a look of sheer terror; how could they keep on playing in the midst of this new attack?

Forlana glanced at them and nodded, sharply.

"GET ON WITH IT" she seemed to be saying.

The piece came to an end and Faye was amazed to discover that the next composition was a pop song from her own world! All the children grinned at the Maestro and began to play this new song with a will, as it was so familiar to them.

Faye could hear Madame Leider's big, operatic tones over all the over vocals, and this struck her as so funny, (for the Professor's voice didn't suit the music at all) that Faye began to giggle... and then she suddenly realised that the happier the music made her, the easier it was to play, and so the happier she became!

It seemed really important that she let the Maestro know of this discovery, but when she looked up at him, she found he was nodding and smiling at her... he already knew, of course he did!

Faye was just about to try and communicate this to Peri, when a massive shock-wave hit the dome, and a very small crack appeared in it, directly over Faye's head!

She continued to play, but soon, she couldn't see her hands because they were obscured... by an evil green mist. Now, she couldn't feel her hands either, so she didn't know if she was still playing or not. She couldn't see the Maestro next.

No! Where was everyone? She was all alone! Why had she dared to think that she could save the Music Fairies? What made her so special?

Faye was a nobody, nothing, talentless... a tear rolled down Faye's cheek as all her old insecurities came back to haunt her.

She swayed, dizzily, and with her last, conscious thought, she cried out what so many of the Music Fairies had, ever since the evil enchantress had come to dwell in the Cacophony Wood...

"I WISH GREENBOW WAS HERE!"

CHAPTER 18

Silence… nothing… darkness…
She'd failed them all.

Faye shivered. Were all the Music Fairies gone? How would she and Peri get home?

A faint touch on her arm nearly made her jump out of her skin. She opened her eyes and turned to see… not Dee Sharp, as she had been expecting, but what seemed to be, through the Woodwind, the figure of… a young woman, a Fairy?
She was taking a seat next to Faye!
Without realising it, Faye took her hands off the keys and heard with relief, the young woman playing in her place!
Although this seemed to take forever, it was actually only a few seconds, and Faye was <u>very</u> relieved to hear that the rest of the orchestra hadn't stopped playing when she had!
The pianist next to her began a new piece; the music was wonderful - full of hope, and Faye felt herself growing happier by the minute.

The Woodwind started to thin out, then drift away and Faye found to her surprise that the Fairy next to her was playing, not on <u>her</u> piano, but a Sotto Voce mat placed on her lap!
Faye smiled at her, and the Fairy smiled back, nodding at the piano.
Faye placed her fingers on the keys again and the two pianists led the orchestra and chorus into a grand, rousing song which every Fairy, who was there as a singer, wove amazing harmonies into, so that they almost drowned out the whole orchestra!
The last of the Woodwind disappeared back through the crack, which immediately sealed itself. Faye glanced up at the Maestro, who was beaming approval at her.

For, not only had the Woodwind dispersed from the dome, it was also drifting <u>away</u> from the dome, back across the Bar Barrier towards Dee Sharp.

Faye could see her face contorted with rage and hatred but couldn't hear her against the might of the orchestra.

On and on they played - tune after tune; sometimes traditional Fairy melodies, sometimes pieces the Maestro or other professors had composed, and even well-known songs from Human composers and songwriters.

Every single member of the orchestra could feel their hearts swelling with pride and the sheer joy of playing music all together.

Faye had never felt such exhilaration and the Fairy next to her seemed to feel it, too, for she played with effortless expertise and Faye was hard to keep up with her!

Suddenly, the Maestro pointed his baton at the Bar Barrier, and glowing silver dots began to appear along its length.

The orchestra cheered and began to play the piece.

As Faye joined in, she suddenly realised what it was... the final movement of the Faye Sonata, when she and Brio had battled the Discords!

Everyone played better and brighter than they ever had before and, with each bar the Woodwind became thinner and thinner... the Bar Barrier began to glow brighter and brighter, and as the music began to build up to the tremendous finale, with Scales hammering out the rhythm on the large timpani drums, a strange light began to gather around Dee Sharp. It built its intensity as the music swelled, and as the final four bars were played it glowed with an eerie red light until, on the final chord, with a tremendous crash of the cymbals, it exploded with such a violent burst of light that all were temporarily blinded, and the music finally ceased.

With everyone blinking and trying to clear their vision, it was a minute or two before they could, at last, see the results of their efforts.

At first, some people gasped in dismay, for the Bar Barrier had been caught in the explosion and pieces of it had been blown apart, with twisted metal making grotesque shapes here and there.

But then, they all noticed what lay <u>beyond</u> the Bar Barrer.

Nothing... The Woodwind was gone; Dee Sharp was gone, and where the old, dead trees had been blasted apart, new grass and shoots just peeked out from the earth, able to reach up to the sun, at last, after so many years of darkness.

After a moment or two of awed silence, as everyone took this in, there was the mightiest cheer that had ever been heard in the whole of Octavia, together with the trumpeting of <u>all</u> the dragons, who had been summoned back just in time to tip the scales in favour of the Music Fairies.

Everyone was so busy hugging each other, laughing, shouting and crying with joy, that only Faye and the Fairy next to her noticed the Maestro stagger slightly.

They rushed over to him, one on either side.

"Maestro! Are you alright? Come and sit down." Faye looked at him, anxiously.

"I'm fine, my dear. Just a little tired."

Faye realised that that was probably a massive understatement, given that he had, for several hours, been holding the entire orchestra and chorus under his control; directing the power of the music where it could do most good.

She went to lead him to her piano stool, so he could rest, but he was busy talking to the Fairy who had so mysteriously appeared, just when most needed.

The Maestro took her hand and bowed.

"Well, my dear, you made it just in time! Thank you."

"Maestro!" She dropped a small curtsey. "It is <u>so</u> good to see you again! Faye called me back - I couldn't have returned here otherwise, as you know."

Faye looked puzzled.

"I… I wished Greenbow was here," she said, confused, "but he didn't come… <u>you</u> turned up instead!"

A delicious pearl of laughter rang out.

"Oh, Faye… I'm sorry, but <u>I'm</u> Greenbow!"

"But I thought…" Faye was cut short by Lee and Dale Van Clef, who had worked their way through the orchestra to swoop the Fairy up and whirl her around, laughing.

"Maestro?" Faye was more confused than ever.

"Let them have their moment," he said. "It is many years since they've all been together."

Faye looked at the trio and noticed, for the first time, that the markings on their wings were all the same.

"Their wings; they're different to the rest of the Fairies?"

"Indeed, they are," replied Monody, a smile on his face.

"But why?" queried Faye.

"They are called Segue's, but that is a <u>long</u> story for a later time," laughed the Composition, "for now, let's go and rejoice that the fight is won, and Octavia is safe, once more!"

Faye nodded, and turned back to her friends who, by this time, were looking around for her.

The next hour was spent talking excitedly about all that had taken place, (as well as making sure Polka was alright and hadn't been affected by the Woodwind, at all!) so that when Faye looked for Greenbow again, she was disappointed to find the fairy had disappeared from view.

CHAPTER 19

The celebrations at the Warehouse lasted long into the night. Having thanked everyone for their commitment, talent and faith in his ability to lead them to victory, the Maestro had sent all the children off in groups to the Mezzo Meadow, under the supervision of Madame Leider and Professor Tamburo, to be returned home, with the promise that they would all be called again soon to be (hopefully) reunited with their own Mentors.

Most of the children were very glad to go, having found the last two days strange and disturbing but, of course, there was no question of Faye and Peri going home that night!

"You two have been very instrumental in this victory," the Maestro told them, "so of course you may stay for the celebrations, but, tomorrow…"

"We know, Maestro," grinned Faye, "we have to go home, because it'll be the third day!"

"Exactly!" he laughed. "Now, go off and enjoy yourselves!"

As they left him, a huge cheer broke out from amongst the Gnomes. Turning to see what had caused this, Faye and Peri saw, in some amusement, that Polka had lost no time once they returned to the Falls, in trying out her brand new kitchen in her brand new home, and was now leading Landler, Presto and Rollo, all bearing heavy baskets, back to the Warehouse.

"How does she do it"? Peri asked, as she and Faye went to help Forlana clear a large table ready for all the food.

"I have no idea!" laughed Forlana. "She's been just the same, ever since we were younglings… always completely obsessed with baking!"

Once all the baskets had been unpacked, everyone sat down and began to eat… and if it was a somewhat strange meal, consisting of what was left of the stew, some raw vegetables and berries, and an assortment of cakes, pastries, pies and loaves, everyone was far too hungry and grateful for anything to eat to complain.

Forlana and Polka were busy chatting and Peri was asking Rollo how he'd managed to make so many masks, so Faye seized the opportunity to ask Landler something that had been worrying her.

"Landler," she began, slowly, "the Maestro didn't… he didn't <u>kill</u> Dee Sharp, did he?"

Landler looked shocked.

"Of course not, Faye! Whatever made you think of such a thing?"

"It's just that, as the music swelled, so did that red light round her, so I thought, maybe…"

"No, Faye," he said, in a more gentle tone. "Dee Sharp did that to herself."

"But how… <u>why</u>?"

"Because," replied Landler with a sigh, "her hatred of everything we stand for grew out of all proportion and, I imagine, once she discovered that Dirge/Dale had deserted her, it tipped her over the edge. She lost all rational thought and the sight of all of <u>us</u>, bonded together in the joy of music, was more than she could bear; her hatred turned inward, and… it destroyed her."

Faye frowned, puzzled by the sadness in Landler's voice.

"It <u>was</u> what we wanted, wasn't it, Landler?"

"Yes," said Landler, slowly, "but I can't forget that she was, originally, a Music Fairy… before her unhappiness turned her into something else."

Faye nodded, silently. She hadn't thought of it like that. Landler was mourning the loss of one of his own, however evil she had become.

"I'm sorry." She laid a hand on his arm. He looked up and smiled at her.

"Now, go and enjoy the party!"

She grabbed Peri and they ran off to dance a jig that the Gnomes (now they'd had some food and a Whoops-A-Daisy or two) had somehow found the energy to play.

Fanfare and Professor Cloche, sometime later, started to oversee groups of Fairies out to the waiting dragons, to begin their homeward journeys, either to Scores Hall or the Red Barn. Fanfare looked much happier and a lot less fussy, (which indeed he was!) having sent Tanto on dragonback, first to Pavane Villa to free all the animals that Landler and Rollo had kept safe in the stables there, so that they could return to their woodland homes nearby, and then to Scores Hall to check on all the magical creatures (including of course, Fanfare's beloved bluebirds and the Inspiration Sprites) to make sure they, too, were safe!

Fanfare had fretted until Tanto returned with the best of good news, and then, dizzy with relief, he had joined in with all the dancing and merriment in a way no one had <u>ever</u> seen before!

Most of the instruments, chairs and music-stands had been ferried back already by the tireless dragons, most of whom had, by now, had the opportunity to speak to Scales. The little dragon was <u>so</u> happy to be reunited with his long lost kin once more, (including his mum and dad, Chromatica and Arpeggio!) that he too, would have flown back and forth all night long, had Monody not stepped in, saying, "If you wish to fly Faye and Peri back to the Mezzo Meadow tomorrow and say goodbye to them, I suggest you get some sleep, now!"

"Ooh! Can I really, Maestro?" The little dragon was surprised and delighted. "I'll go and sleep now, shall I?"

"Yes, please… and Scales," Monody called after him, as he made his way to the lean-to, "<u>very</u> well done, today."

"Thank you, Maestro!" He gave a funny little bow, then trotted off, happily.

By the time the only folk left were the residence of Cadence Falls and the Maestro's team, Shawm and Dal passed lighted candles around, and everyone formed a line either side of the pathway that led to the little green, where the cherry tree grew, which lay just before the Gnomes back gardens.

Dash, Lilt and Sackbut slowly and carefully carried the boulders that had once been Crumhorn, and laid them in the centre of the green.

The Maestro, himself, followed them, then turned to the crowd and said, "Here lies Crumhorn, a fallen hero. He gave his life to save another. Let us always remember him with affection and honour, every time we pass by his resting place."

Several of the Fairies had gathered up every flower not damaged by the Woodwind, and now came to place them around the boulders, so that, already, the place had a look of peace and tranquillity about it, in the moonlight.

The ceremony over, the Fairies and Gnomes began to head for home, saying goodnight to each other, and bowing respectfully to the place where Crumhorn lay.

Sackbut, looking a little lost, was about to head back to his usual corner in the Warehouse, when Dash said, "No, Sackbut, you come back to mine."

"Really?" The Goblin's eyes were big; his ears large and knobbly once more, now that Dee Sharp's magic had gone.

"Yes," Dash said, firmly. "You're one of us, now."

Dash and Lilt set off up the hill with Sackbut between them.

"You look happy," Landler said, softly, as Polka smiled after them.

"I am... that's as it should be. He's won his place here in Cadence Falls now, hasn't he, dearest?"

"Yes, he has." Landler took her hand. "Home, now?"

"Indeed!!" She grinned at him, "I have a kitchen to clear up!"

He laughed. "That can wait til tomorrow!"

They said goodnight to the others, then set off to their new home.

"I hope you don't mind all cramming into mine tonight," laughed Forlana, "but it <u>is</u> their first night in their new home!"

"Of course!" cried the girls.

"Rollo can stay at mine," said Presto, calling a cheery goodnight as he hauled Rollo off up the hill.

"Maestro?" Forlana gave him her arm.

"Thank you, Forlana - I <u>will</u> take the offer of a comfy chair for the night, if I may?"

"<u>Chair</u>, indeed! After all the work <u>you</u> put in today, you'll have my bed, and <u>I'll</u> have the chair!"

Monody pretended to look scared.

"I wouldn't dare disagree with you, my dear!"

The girls laughed and the merry party headed towards the double hills, calling goodnight to the stragglers heading home, as they went.

CHAPTER 20

The next morning, Presto and Rollo joined the girls for breakfast at Forlana's.

"What I <u>still</u> don't understand…" Forlana was saying as she went to open the door to the others, " … is why we've said, time and time again, that we needed Greenbow here, and she never came, but the minute <u>Faye</u> says it… she turns up!"

The Maestro waited until Presto and Rollo had each been handed a cup of Lupin tea, before answering.

"The reason is simple." He looked at them, one by one, before finally resting his gaze on Faye. "She needed to be called by a Human, not a Fairy."

Five pairs of eyes stared at him in amazement.

"But… if you knew that, Maestro, why didn't you <u>tell</u> Faye?" stammered Forlana.

"Because," he said, slowly, "the rules governing Segues are very strict, and known only to those who can treat the knowledge responsibly."

There were puzzled glances all around the table and nobody realised they were all waiting for more information. (Faires knew that Segues existed in Octavia but did not know the evolution of what happens.)

"What <u>is</u> a Segue?" Faye asked, remembering her conversation with the Maestro the day before.

"I'll tell you as much as I can… as much as I am <u>allowed</u>," he amended.

He placed the tips of his fingers together; a sure sign, to those who knew him, that he was concentrating on what to say.

"As you know," he began, "we call children with musical ability into our world, from time to time, to help us. <u>Children</u>," he stressed, "because Children have the capability to believe in magical things."

Faye and Peri nodded.

"But children grow up - they become adults, and their belief is replaced with the cares and burdens of the Human world, and so they forget how to believe."

He held his hand up, as the two girls shook their heads.

"<u>Most</u> adults cease to believe," he amended. "However, from time to time, an adult somehow manages to not only believe, but to have memories of their visits here. Sometimes these fade over time, or the person convinces themselves that they only imagined it but rarely, some Humans return to us... as adults!"

He looked at the two girls to see if they understood.

"Like Lee and Dale!" They both said at once.

He nodded, smiling.

"If this happens, they are offered a choice; they can hand their Clef Crystals back and be returned to their own world, with <u>no</u> memory of Octavia at all, or..." He looked at Faye and Peri, "they can make a one-way trip - a Segue, which means a continuation, into Octavia and live out their lives here, but they can never return to the Human world again."

There was a pause while everyone around the table digested this information, which was news to them.

"So..." began Forlana, "Lee and Dale were originally Humans, but chose to Segue here as adults... so, why do they have wings?" she asked.

"So as to blend in with the Fairy folk here, and to make the transition as smooth as possible. However, <u>their</u> wings have unusual markings down the edges; no one knows why, but I suspect it was something to do with the Segue - they are neither completely Human nor Fairy. As a matter of fact, their wings do not work as well as a true Fairy's... they are mainly for show. Lee and Dale lost their parents when they were quite young men, and had no other family, so when they were offered the chance to live here permanently, they jumped at it. They still age, and will eventually die, but they will have a much longer life here."

Faye suddenly thought of something important, something that had bothered her before.

"But, Maestro, Lee and Dale are <u>much</u> older than Greenbow, yet they greeted her as an old friend! How can that be?"

The Maestro rose from the table. "That is not my tale to tell," he said cryptically. "But I suspect you will find out soon, anyway," he whispered in her ear, as he passed behind her on his way to the window.

"Ah! It is time to leave, my dears." He smiled, then went to open the front door.

Faye and Peri walked outside, then stopped short, staring.

Every inch of the street was covered in Fairies and Gnomes who all set up a great cheer as soon as they saw the two girls.

Faye turned, wide-eyed to the Maestro who shrugged and grinned.

"I've been with you!" he said, pretending no knowledge of the crowd. (It had, in fact, all been arranged by Ocarina and Marcato, the previous evening!)

Suddenly, a trumpet sounded in the distance and over the crest of the nearest hill, came Scales, Landler and Polka walking either side of him.

The little dragon stopped right outside Forlana's cottage, and Landler and Polka came to help the two girls up onto his back. Once they were settled, Scales turned to face the crowd. Landler then stepped back to stand next to the Maestro, so the girls could see him.

"The whole village of Cadence Falls wishes me to publicly thank Faye and Peri for saving them from Dee Sharp, the Woodwind… and any evil in the foreseeable future! We are all very grateful to you."

Everyone, as if on cue, bowed low to the girls including, to Faye's embarrassment, Maestro Monody!

They said, 'thank you' in small voices, then Presto, deciding to put them out of their misery, yelled "MUSIC!" at the top of his lungs and the Gnomes struck up a merry jig as Scales began to walk proudly down through the village towards the Mezzo Meadow.

All at once, the air was full of flying, laughing Fairies, swirling and somersaulting around their heads.

"I'd almost forgotten they could fly," whispered Peri, entranced by all the dazzling wings that fluttered around them.

They were suddenly joined by much larger wings.

"Brio!" cried Faye, as her Beamer friend hovered overhead.

"I am here," he thought to her.

She smiled and waved up at him, then suddenly, Scales took off and followed Brio in flight!

"Um… is he supposed to do that?" asked Peri.

"Not sure," replied Faye, but then Brio 'spoke' to her again.

"It is well - look down."

Faye nodded, then tapped Peri's shoulder and pointed downwards.

Below them, sparkling in the sunlight was the Pizzicato Pool, and rising out of the water, in a great crowd, was virtually every Ondulandi who lived there... including Solenne, the new Olani!

All were playing their harps, and <u>all</u>, as Scales swooped low over the water, cried in clear, but strange voices, "Fai-ee! Fai-ee! Per-ee! Per-ee!" over and over again.

Peri, who knew how extremely rare it was for the Ondulandi to name any outsider, thought that she <u>must</u> remember to tell Faye what a huge honour that had been!

Eventually, Scales set them down at the edge of the Mezzo Meadow, said his goodbyes and flew a little way off to bask in the sun.

Most of the Fairies and Gnomes had peeled away once Scales had taken flight, and any that <u>had</u> come to see them off, now stood respectfully to one side, while the Maestro's group said goodbye to each other.

Presto and Rollo gave the girls a quick hug each, saying, "Well done... and thank you!"

They went to join the group waiting at the edge of the Meadow.

Faye and Peri turned to their respective Mentors.

Landler looked at them both with pride.

"Faye, Peri, you have both done <u>so</u> much more than we dared hope; you have freed us, and you take with you our undying gratitude."

Polka came to grasp both of Peri's hands.

"Thank you so much for getting the Diapason Plant! If you hadn't..."

"Oh, for goodness sake!" broke in a familiar voice. "Anyone would think you were never going to see them again! Listen, when you come back, we really must begin your training properly, without all these interruptions!"

At Forlana's words, Monody burst out laughing.

"I think, my dear Forlana, that these events of the last six months may be classed as slightly more than 'interruptions'!"

"Oh well, you know what I mean," Forlana began, but the two girls suddenly both gave her a hug, at once.

"You mean we're coming back?"

"Isn't it over?"

"Of course it isn't over!" the Fairy replied, briskly turning away to hide her emotion.

Monody came to her rescue.

"No, indeed! There are still many things you will be able to help us with, I hope, although it may not be quite as exciting, I fear!"

"As long as we can come back, I don't care how boring it is!" said Peri, tactless in her excitement.

Landler and Polka laughed and whilst Peri was distracted, the Maestro murmured quietly to Faye, "Greenbow asked me to give you this, and said you will understand, soon."

He slipped a small, silver ring into her hand; she looked at it and saw it was engraved with tiny leaves and flowers, surrounding a treble clef. Faye slipped it on - it fit her middle finger perfectly!

"I was hoping to see her afterwards, Maestro, … " she began.

"I know," Monody replied gently, "but having had such a rough transition here, I made Fanfare take her straight back to Scores Hall, where the Medics can take care of her and make sure she's alright."

"Will she stay here, now?" asked Faye.

"Yes. She'll stay."

Faye nodded. Maybe she'd get to see her next time.

He bent down to whisper in her ear, "You understand, the music is the magic! You won the battle for us!"

"Also," he continued smoothly, as Forlana looked over at them, "Fanfare asked me to say goodbye and to tell you that his bluebirds… and all the Sprites are now on the mend!"

"Oh, thank goodness!"

Landler came up to them. "Are you ready, Maestro?"

"Yes, indeed!"

The two girls made their way into the centre of the Meadow, turned to face the others, and held up their Clef Crystals in front of them.

"We'll see you both again… very soon!" said Maestro Monody. "Remember, the music is the magic!"

"We will!" They both cried, as the Composition Magician's had hovered over the Rubato Stone, and all their friends waved goodbye.

CHAPTER 21

Epilogue

Faye and Peri barely had time to register that they were back in Faye's front room, when Jenny Martin came in.

"Oh, Faye! I'm sorry to interrupt your practise, but..." she swallowed hard, "I've just had a call from the Home and... Aunt Laura died during the night!"

Faye gasped. She knew Aunt Laura hadn't been well, in fact, they hadn't been allowed to visit for the previous two Sundays, but she hadn't expected this!

Both girls went to Jenny and led her to the sofa, as she was so obviously shaken up.

Faye whispered to Peri, "Can you sit with her, while I go and make some tea?"

"Of course!" replied Peri. Faye disappeared into the kitchen.

"I'm so sorry, Mrs Martin," Peri said, gently.

"It's silly, really," said Jenny, dabbing at her eyes with a tissue. "She's not even <u>my</u> aunt! It's just that she was my last contact with Kieran," (Kieran was the name of Faye's dad, who had died when she was little.) "She was <u>his</u> aunt and would tell me stories of when he was a boy - things I never knew about him."

Peri nodded. Faye had told her best friend how guilty she sometimes felt that she couldn't really remember her dad.

"And, of course," Jenny continued, more to herself than Peri, "she was so good to us - paying for Faye's piano lessons and... er... other things..." She faltered suddenly, not wishing to share with her daughters' best friend the number of times Aunt Laura had come to her rescue when the bills threatened to overwhelm her.

Luckily, Faye came back just then with a cup of tea.

"Here, drink this, Mum."

"Oh, thank you, Faye."

She smiled at her capable daughter, as she sipped her tea.

"Er… would you like me to go, now?" Peri suddenly thought perhaps they'd rather be alone.

Surprisingly, Jenny Martin said, "No. Please stay, Peri. You're Faye's best friend and she needs you. Also…" she got up, "I've just remembered something… a few weeks ago, when Aunt Laura first became ill, she gave me a letter and said that I'd know when the time was right to give it to you."

She crossed to the mantelpiece and, from underneath a pile of bills and bank statements, took out a lilac envelope.

"I think that time is now; here it is." She handed it to Faye with a sniff.

Just then the phone rang. "Now, who can *that* be?"

Jenny went into the kitchen to answer it.

Faye turned the envelope over… and made a discovery.

"Peri, Look! It's addressed to both of us!"

"What?" Peri looked down, and, sure enough, in Aunt Laura's neat copperplate writing were the names Faye and Peri!

With gathering excitement Faye tore it open and pulled out the crisp folded pages. Something fluttered to the floor, but, in their haste to read the letter, the girls didn't notice.

Heads together, they opened the first page:

"My dear Faye and Peri," Great-Aunt Laura began, "for some time now it has been apparent that you have wished to ask me questions about certain things that have happened over the last few months."

Faye and Peri glanced at each other, excitedly.

"I would have loved to tell you all I knew, but the rules governing these things are <u>very</u> strict, and I didn't want to jeopardise <u>your</u> adventures or, indeed, mine!

However, events are coming to a point where I feel that I may, <u>now</u>, be allowed to answer at least <u>some</u> of your questions.

As a young girl, it was discovered that I had some talent for the Piano…"

"That's putting it mildly!" said Faye. Aunt Laura had been a renowned Concert Pianist in her day.

"Shhh!" said Peri. "Keep reading!"

Faye grinned at her and went on.

"For my 10th birthday, my grandmother gave me a necklace and told me, very quietly, just before she left, to wear it when I practised.

I did so… and you can imagine what happened…"

Faye and Peri gasped.

"I was fortunate to have many friends, but three of them, in particular, I grew very close to, when we discovered, by chance, that we all had something <u>very</u> important in common... the Music Fairies!"

Faye nearly dropped the letter in surprise.

"I knew it!" cried Peri, grabbing the letter to stop it falling. "I <u>told</u> you she knew!"

Faye was too amazed to say anything, so Peri took over reading it aloud.

"At the Conservatoire where I studied, I met two young men who were also gifted musicians... the Van Clef brothers: Lee and Dale."

Faye gasped again, but Peri kept on reading.

"Tony Tonal and I had been friends ever since we both had the same piano teacher as children, but, alas, his eyesight had begun to weaken, even then, so he did not attend the Conservatoire with me.

Our music brought us together, but it wasn't until we <u>all</u> accidentally met each other in Octavia, that we realised we'd <u>all</u> been helping the Music Fairies since we were children!

Once we knew this, it was wonderful to be able to have long conversations about all our adventures there and talk openly about Fairies without anyone thinking we were mad!

Although we were nearly grown up, we'd never stopped believing and so we were able to go back, time and time again, for years, during which time Lee, Dale, and myself graduated from the Conservatoire, and went our separate ways. Although Tony and I stayed in touch, the brothers went off to begin <u>their</u> musical careers and so, unless we bumped into them in Octavia, we didn't hear of them for quite a while.

Then, one day, the Maestro (Not <u>your</u> Maestro... he was not yet ready to be appointed, then) told me that Lee and Dale's parents had died in a plane crash. They had no other family, and after a long conversation with him, where he was forced to tell them that there <u>was</u> a way in which they could stay in Octavia, they had both requested to become Segues.

I was very surprised, because they were so young... and it's a decision that can only be made once.

The Maestro, of course, would have told me <u>none</u> of this, but for the fact that it was going to affect myself, and Tony, too.

The problem, the Maestro explained, was that if <u>we</u> kept returning to Octavia, it would remind the brothers of all they had left behind in the Human world and so would make the transition much harder for them.

We had a choice to make: either become Segues ourselves, or make this our last visit to Octavia!

It was <u>very</u> hard, but Tony had just become engaged; Lionel and I had been married for two years... and I had my career; there was no question of our leaving!

We had to agree to strict conditions. We <u>would</u> be allowed to retain our memories of Octavia <u>and</u> our Clef Crystals, but only if we promised never to speak of any of it, unless we had positive proof that someone else had also seen the Music Fairies.

To be honest, Faye, I feel I may have broken the rules slightly, by being so insistent that you wear the Clef Crystal <u>at</u> <u>all</u> <u>times</u> when you practised, but I was so eager for you to have your share of all the adventures that I <u>knew</u> were waiting for you! (I would, of course, have given the Crystal to dear Kieran, your father, but he was the most <u>un</u>musical person I'd ever met!)

To continue, after you returned from your first visit to Octavia, I was desperate to ask you about it, but was unsure how you would react to an old lady asking you about Fairyland!

How I wish I had, though when you returned the second time, and were so ill, I racked my brains for a way in which I could help you - I even considered wearing the Clef Crystal <u>myself</u> to see if I could get back to Octavia to ask for help! I didn't know <u>what</u> was wrong, but I knew, somehow, that the answer must lie there... and then I met Peri.

What a wonderful friend you have there, Faye.

Always reassure this friendship - it will last a lifetime, I'm sure.

I couldn't just come out and <u>tell</u> Peri what I wanted her to do, but she's such a clever girl that I knew she'd figure it all out!

When I noticed that Peri had a Clef Crystal of her own, I decided I would speak to you both, when the time was right... but now, I'm afraid, that time has run out. It is my greatest hope that I will, somehow, be allowed back into Octavia, (maybe looking somewhat better than I do, now!) and, If I <u>am</u>, I <u>so</u> hope to see both of you there!

Enjoy your adventures - it is so much more fun when you have a friend to share them with! As you grow up, try to <u>always</u> remember Octavia and the Music Fairies!

With much love, I remain forever your (Great) Aunt Laura."

Peri put the letter down and took Faye's hand.

"You see?" she said, gently, "she knew all along - she just couldn't tell us about it, until we found out for ourselves."

Faye nodded; a big lump in her throat. She so wished she could have told Aunt Laura all about their adventures… and now, it was too late.

She rubbed her eyes and was about to fold the letter up and put it back in the envelope, when her mum suddenly came back in and sat, with a jerk, on the sofa - looking completely bewildered.

"What's wrong, Mum?" asked Faye, worried.

"Nothing… no, nothing really. It's just…" she paused and looked at the girls.

"That was Aunt Laura's solicitor on the phone. He wants me to go to his office next week to discuss Aunt Laura's Will."

Faye nodded, having a vague notion that a Will was something that old people wrote before they died.

"Faye," Jenny took her daughter's hand. "Aunt Laura has left us everything… by everything, I mean all her things, her piano, all her music for you… and… all her money!"

Jenny drew a deep breath.

"The solicitor said he couldn't 'discuss numbers' over the phone, but he did say we'll never need to worry about money again!"

She swallowed hard.

"Aunt Laura also set up a trust fund for you… to study music when you're older… if you want to?"

"Oh, I want to!" cried Faye, hardly daring to believe any of this could be true.

Mother and daughter stared at each other in happy disbelief, and Peri, feeling it really was time to see if someone could come and pick her up, got off the sofa… then noticed something under Faye's feet. She bent down and picked it up.

"This must have fallen out when you opened the letter, Faye."

Faye looked at the old photo in Peri's hand. It was of four young people standing outside a grand old building, which must be the Music Conservatoire Aunt Laura had spoken of in her letter.

Faye's mum leaned over her shoulder and said, "That's Aunt Laura, there, and I think those must be the friends she spoke of so often. See? There's Mr Tonal, our piano tuner - she's known him for years!"

Indeed, the tall, lean (and much younger) figure of Tony Tonal, holding up a white stick, smiled up out of the photo at her. He must have gone to visit Aunt Laura, she supposed.

There, too, were Lee and Dale Van Clef, again, looking very much younger, but still recognisable.

As one, Faye and Peri looked, finally, at the young woman in the photo, then turned to each other in joyful understanding - for there, looking up at them, was a face they had seen only recently.

She wore a cheese-cloth smock, flared trousers and clogs. Faye could just make out a ring on her little finger… and, tying back her long, light brown hair was…

A Green Bow.

NOTES FROM THE AUTHOR

There were a few notes written in the back of the second notepad that book 6 was written in. I feel like they are important notes for you as readers, to know, as they may help to explain a few things.
These are written word for word as mum wrote them:

The time-limit for Humans to spend in Octavia is 3 <u>complete</u> days! We discount the day on which they arrive as, for some obscure reason, most Humans tend to arrive in the afternoon!
The only time this is <u>not</u> applicable is the very <u>first</u> time they are called. This is because the pull of the Fairy world has had no chance to take hold.
Indeed, it is possible that, though they never spent more than 3 days there at a time, Dale and Lee came so often, that the pull of Octavia became stronger than that of their own world, which is why they chose to Segue.

The 'once in a lifetime' choice to Segue is particularly applicable to Great Aunt Laura.
At the exact same moment that Faye called for Greenbow - Laura was drawing her final breath.
Her spirit was literally pulled into Octavia, as her body died in the Human world.
It would be expected that, eventually, her spirit would fade away, but not for a long time, as she is so attuned to the Music Fairies.

Printed in Great Britain
by Amazon